Chana

Book

Select Books by Ashok K. Banker

RAMAYANA SERIES

Prince of Ayodhya
Siege of Mithila
Demons of Chitrakut
Armies of Hanuman
Bridge of Rama
King of Ayodhya
Vengeance of Ravana
Sons of Sita

MAHABHARATA SERIES

The Forest of Stories
The Seeds of War
The Children of Midnight
The Darkness Before Dawn
The Eclipse of Dharma
The Sons of Misrule
The Kingdom of Beasts

ITIHASA SERIES

Ten Kings
Ashoka: Lion of Maurya
Ashoka: Satrap of Taxila
*Ashoka: Master of Magadha**
*Shivaji**

CRIME NOVELS

The Iron Bra
Murder & Champagne
Ten Dead Admen
Blood Red Sari
Burnt Saffron Sky
Silver Acid Rain
Rust Black Heart

ROMANCE

*Love Stories from the
    Mahabharata*
Bombay Times

SCIENCE FICTION

Gods of War
Vortal: Shockwave
Awaken

SHORT FICTION

*My Father Drank My Lover
    and other stories*

---

* *Forthcoming*

Chanakya
Book 1

ASHOK K. BANKER

First published by Westland Publications Private Limited in 2018
61, 2nd Floor, Silverline Building, Alapakkam Main Road,
Maduravoyal, Chennai 600095

Westland and the Westland logo are the trademarks of Westland
Publications Private Limited, or its affiliates.

Copyright © Ashok K. Banker, 2018

ISBN: 9789387578166

10 9 8 7 6 5 4 3 2 1

This is a work of fiction. Names, characters, organisations, places,
events and incidents are either products of the author's imagination
or used fictitiously.

Typeset by Jojy Philip

Printed at Thomson Press (I) Ltd.

For every young mind that dares to question, seek, explore.
Never stop. Never get discouraged. Never give up.
True genius accumulates from the persistent pursuit
of knowledge.
We are each Chanakya in our own special way.

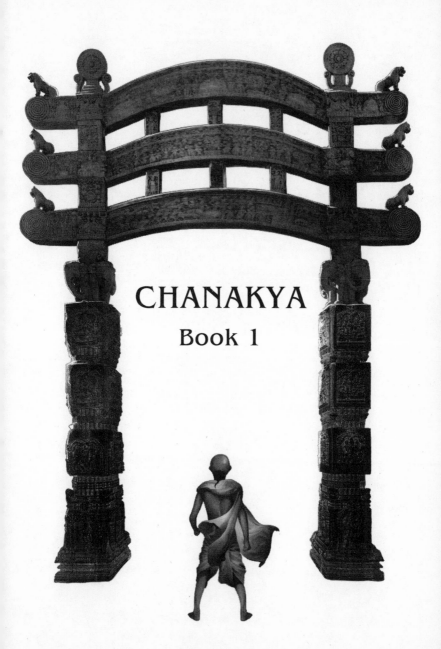

CHANAKYA
Book 1

1

The class was chanting its Sanskrit grammar when Vishnu arrived.

He came from the direction of the lake, sauntering as if he had all the time in the world. The single pigtail dangling from the back of his bald head bobbed and bounced from side to side. His white dhoti seemed fairly clean which was unusual, but as he came closer it was apparent that he had gotten soaking wet at some point; the garment was yet to dry out fully. He was otherwise dressed exactly like all the other little brahmacharyas seated cross-legged in the open-air class beneath the peepal tree: Above the white cotton dhoti, his upper body was bare except for the sacred thread hanging diagonally over his shoulder and passing around his waist.

He was eating a small yellowish-green ber as he walked. It was early in the season and the ber was barely ripe and very sour. Each time he took a small bite, he screwed up his face and squeezed his eyes shut; he then opened them slowly, jaw moving from side to side as if to mitigate the sour taste. He would then swallow and open his mouth and eyes wide, expressing his delight.

The chanting children began to nudge each other as they caught sight of him. By the time he went through this ber-eating performance the third time, every pair of eyes in the class was watching him. Several paused mid-chant to emit small, involuntary giggles. When Vishnu realised he had finished his last ber, he stopped, just behind the peepal tree beneath which the teacher sat, reciting the conjugations that the class was repeating after him. Vishnu went through an elaborate pantomime of trying to decide whether to go back to fetch more ber, tapping his foot on the ground while tapping his finger on the side of his head and turning to glance the way he had come. When he finally threw up his hands in apparent helplessness and turned back, the class burst out into loud laughter.

The sight that elicited this extreme reaction was the large red stain on the rear of Vishnu's dhoti, formed perfectly in the exact shape of his two little buttocks.

At the explosion of laughter, the teacher frowned at his class. He noted the direction of their gazes and turned to look at the object of their amusement.

When he saw the mud-stained rear of Vishnu's dhoti, he sighed and shook his head.

'Vishnu Gupta,' he called out in a patient but firm voice.

The muddy dhoti stopped.

The little pigtail bobbed, exchanging places with an innocent little face as Vishnu turned his head around.

An "uh oh" look appeared on that face.

'Yes, guruji?' he said.

'Do you know what time pupils are expected to arrive at the gurukul?'

'Yes, guruji.'

'And can you see that it is well past that expected time?'

'Yes, guruji.'

'Then why are you late for gurukul, Vishnu Gupta?'

The chotti on the bald head bobbed as the little face shook from side to side.

'Guruji, I am not late for gurukul,' Vishnu said.

The teacher frowned. 'You are not?'

'No, guruji.'

'All the students are here, I am here, the sun is high in the sky. How can you say you are not late?'

'Because of you, guruji.'

A few involuntary smiles came from the brahmacharyas, quickly covered by their hands.

'Explain what you mean, Vishnu.'

'Guruji, you had said we had to learn the first Paksha of Mandala Seven by the end of this week.'

'Yes, I did.'

'Then I put up my hand.' Vishnu raised his right hand to demonstrate, revealing the half-eaten ber still clutched in his palm.

A small round of titters began but subsided immediately, suppressed by little hands.

'And you said "What is it now, Vishnu Gupta?"' He imitated the teacher's voice perfectly, drawing another round of titters, also suppressed.

The teacher sighed and nodded. 'Yes, I recall.'

'And I asked you "Guruji, when can we go and play?" And you said—'

The teacher cut in quickly before Vishnu could imitate him again. 'I said you could go play when you had finished learning the first Paksha of Mandala Seven. I recall that as well. What is your point, Vishnu Gupta?'

'Well, guruji, I finished learning, so I was playing.'

The teacher looked around his class and then looked at Vishnu. 'I see. That instruction was meant for the entire class,

Vishnu, not only you. But I see what you are saying. You finished learning the first Paksha of Mandala Seven, so you thought you were free to go play instead of attending gurukul; is that what you meant?'

'Yes, guruji.'

'Well, you were mistaken. We are not here to learn just the first Paksha of Mandala Seven, we are here to learn the entire Mandala Seven and I would like us to finish learning it before we break for the holidays.'

'Yes, guruji. I understand.'

'If you understand so much then why did you miss gurukul today?'

'Because I finished learning it before the holidays.'

'Yes, you said that already. You finished the first Paksha, but we still have the rest of Mandala Seven, as I just explained. So if you would kindly—'

'No, guruji,' Vishnu Gupta said.

The teacher sighed again, a patient long-suffering expression on his face. 'What do you mean, "No"?'

'I did not just do that, guruji. I knew that it would not be enough to only study Paksha One of Mandala Seven. So I studied it all.'

The teacher raised his eyebrows, his eyes widening. 'You studied the whole of Mandala Seven all by yourself?'

'No, guruji.'

The teacher frowned. 'What do you mean, "No"? You just said that you studied it all.'

'Yes, guruji. But not just all of Mandala Seven.'

The teacher squinted at Vishnu. 'Then what did you mean?'

'I studied it all. All the Mandalas.'

The teacher stared at him, his mouth opening slowly. He gaped openly for a moment. The sound of a cow mooing in the shed next to the gurukul broke him out of his reverie. He shut his mouth slowly and attempted to recover his composure.

He peered at Vishnu as if he had suddenly turned into some unfamiliar creature with too many heads.

'You studied *all* the Mandalas of the first Parva?'

'No, guruji. I studied the whole Rig Veda,' Vishnu said cheerfully. He stole a glance at the ber in his hand as if it were calling to him to *eat me, eat me now; remember how yummy I am!*

The teacher stood up slowly, his mouth dropping open again. This time it stayed open even after the cow mooed loudly again from the shed. 'The whole...' He shook his head slowly. 'That is impossible. It takes years to master the Rig Veda. I myself...' He shook his head. 'And all by yourself? It is quite impossible.'

'Guruji, shall I recite it for you?' Vishnu asked eagerly. And without waiting for the teacher to speak, he launched into the first Paksha of the first Mandala of the first Parva, reciting it with rote perfection, every intonation, nuance, stress and syllable.

All the tittering stopped; every brahmacharya in the gurukul listened with rapt attention. Even the older brahmacharyas who had been tending to the livestock and other chores came to listen, nudging one another as their eyes grew big and round too.

The guru broke in at last. 'Enough. Very well. So you have learned the padapad well. But it is not enough to simply recite the text. Learning the meaning of each shloka is equally important for a brahmin.'

'Yes, guruji,' Vishnu said, 'Which shloka would you like me to interpret?'

The teacher stared at his little pupil for a long moment as if he had sprouted more heads, in addition to the several he was already sporting. Finally he shrugged and said, 'The one hundred and fifty-first shloka of Mandala Nine.'

Vishnu instantly launched into an explanation of the shloka his teacher had named.

The older brahmacharyas stared at each other, eyes even wider and rounder.

The teacher lowered his head, defeated. He raised his hand to attract Vishnu's attention.

'Yes, guruji?' Vishnu asked eagerly. 'Would you like me to continue reciting or would you like me to continue interpreting the shlokas?'

'Neither,' the guru said, his voice hollow, 'You have my permission to go play.' He paused, then added, 'Do whatever you wish, Vishnu Gupta.'

Vishnu joined his palms together and bent forward from the waist. 'Thank you, guruji. Pranaam.'

Then he turned and continued up the path again. His chotti danced on the back of his little bald head. He popped the ber into his mouth and crunched it loudly. The mud stain on the back of his dhoti appeared to jiggle as he bounced and hopped on his way, humming a happy tune as he went.

2

That evening, after Vishnu returned home, washed himself and sat for the evening meal with his parents and sisters, his father looked at him and said, 'Vishnu Gupta.'

'Yes, father,' he replied promptly.

'I heard today that you were showing off in class again.'

'I wasn't showing off, father, I was only answering guruji's questions.'

'That's not what I heard,' his father said, pulling up his legs to sit comfortably on the simple mud floor. 'I heard you were reciting the Rig Veda and interpreting it as well.'

'Yes, father,' Vishnu replied, 'but only because teacher asked me to do so.'

His father looked at him intently, 'Teacher suddenly decided to ask you to recite and interpret the Rig Veda, for no cause at all?'

Vishnu Gupta stuck out his tongue and immediately covered his mouth. His sisters, who had been swivelling their heads from their brother to their father, giggled. 'No, father,' he said softly. 'He only asked because I told him I had learned the complete Rig Veda.'

Rishi Gupta continued to look intently at his son. 'And why did you feel it was necessary to inform him of this fact?'

'Because he thought I had not learned my lessons for this week.'

'And why would he think that?'

Vishnu Gupta shrugged, knowing he had run out room to manoeuvre further. 'Because I did not attend gurukul today.'

Rishi Gupta nodded slowly, 'I thought as much. What did I tell you the last time you missed gurukul, Vishnu Gupta?'

'"Never miss another lesson,"' Vishnu sang out, imitating his father's voice perfectly, except for the bass intonation which his pre-pubescent vocal cords could not achieve.

His sisters giggled into their hands. Vishnu's mother stood in the doorway, listening as she finished her evening chores.

'And yet you missed gurukul,' Rishi Gupta said.

Vishnu shrugged. 'You said not to miss another lesson. I had already learned that lesson and the rest of my lessons for this season.'

Rishi Gupta nodded as if he had expected a response along these lines. 'Let me make it explicitly clear then: No more missing gurukul again. You will attend every class and pay full attention to your guru, whatever the lesson. You will do whatever is expected of you in class, be it reciting shlokas or learning nirukta. Do you follow me?'

'Yes, father,' Vishnu said.

'Good.' His father rose to go into the other room.

Vishnu's three sisters, all elder to him, came over and poked fingers into his sides. His eldest sister flicked his chotti with her finger. 'Show-off! Show-off! Show-off!' they chanted softly, teasing him.

Vishnu giggled uncontrollably, rolling on to his back to try and avoid their fingers. 'Stop it! It tickles!'

They tickled him even more relentlessly, till he was rolling and squirming helplessly.

'He's much smarter than all the other brahmacharyas,' Vishnu's mother said in the other room to his father. 'It's only understandable if his mind wanders from schoolwork.'

'He's much smarter than even the teacher,' Rishi Gupta said as he settled in for the evening. 'That doesn't mean he should simply stop going to gurukul.'

'But he already learns everything just by listening and talking to you,' she said. 'Does it really matter if he misses a few days here and there?'

He looked at her affectionately. 'You always stand up for him. I understand that. But it's not about learning. It's about socialising and blending in.'

'Blending in?' She shook her head. 'Our Vishnu?' She laughed softly.

He smiled. 'Yes, I know. He stands out like an elephant in a herd of deer. But that's what worries me so much, Vishnu's mother. He attracts too much attention to himself. It will make him swollen-headed as time goes by.'

She sat beside him. 'I don't understand your concern. Our only son is a prodigy, a genius. Someone with his intelligence comes along once in generations, you said.'

'And I meant it,' he replied, 'I still mean it.'

'Then he's bound to stand out from ordinary boys. It's only natural.'

'Yes, but it's one thing to stand out in a certain situation where he has to use his intellect for some purpose, and quite another thing to simply show off just to get his own way.'

'Ah,' she said, 'I see the problem. You're afraid he will misuse his genius to get out of situations. Like he did today to avoid attending gurukul.'

'Exactly,' he said warmly.

'But my beloved Vishnu's father,' she said sweetly, 'if he

can't use his great intelligence to get what he wants from life, then what good is it being so intelligent?'

He stared at her.

She raised her eyebrows. 'Well?'

'You make a good point,' he said.

'Of course I do,' she said, smiling, 'I'm Vishnu Gupta's mother, aren't I?'

3

Vaishali was in the woods, collecting sticks for the fire when she saw the familiar little chotti bouncing along. She put down her sticks at the foot of a mango tree and ran to the path.

'Vishnu!' she cried as she came up beside him, breathless from running too fast. 'Ouch, I have stitch in my side.'

Vishnu continued up the path.

'Will you wait a moment,' she cried out, 'I ran too fast and now….' She wiggled and twisted till the stitch worked its way out of her side.

Vishnu was several yards up the path, walking along as if he hadn't encountered her at all.

'Vishnu Gupta!' she said, 'stop and listen when a lady wants to talk to you.'

'You're no lady,' he said, running faster, 'you're just a girl.'

'Same thing,' she said, trying to catch up with him. 'It's only polite.'

She finally caught up with him where the path turned sharply down toward the creek. She put her hands on her waist, scowling at him. 'You're supposed to be so smart, but you don't know anything.'

He stopped abruptly. 'I know the whole Rig Veda.'

'So what?' she said.

'Do you know the whole Rig Veda?' he asked indignantly, 'do you even know one Mandala of the Rig Veda? Even one shloka?'

'That's going too far,' she said, wagging a finger in warning. 'My father is the teacher of our village. I know a lot of shlokas!'

Vishnu folded his arms on his chest and stuck out his chin. 'I know the whole Rig Veda,' he said haughtily, 'And now I'm learning the Yajur Veda.'

'So what?' she said. 'Many people know the Vedas. All four of them. Even the Mahabharata, which is known as the Fifth Veda. See, even I know that.'

'Grown-up people,' he said. 'Not other seven-year-olds. I'm seven years old.'

'I know that too,' she said, 'I'm eight. My eighth naming day was last month. Which makes me older than you. Which means I'm your elder. You should respect your elders.'

He frowned. 'You're only elder to me by a few months. I'll turn eight in a few months too.'

'Yes, but I'm eight now. So respect your elder. Let me go swimming with you.'

He sighed heavily, a long-suffering sigh, and shook his head firmly. He unfolded his hands and started to walk forward, but Vaishali blocked his way. She was a little taller than him. Vishnu was short for his age.

'Move,' he said.

'I'm coming with you,' she said.

'No.'

'Am too.'

'Are not.'

'Am.'

'Not.'

'I won't let you go then. Take me with you or I won't let you pass.'

He tried to take a step forward but she stood in his path. He tried to dodge to one side; she dodged with him. Every move he tried, she countered him. She was aided by the fact that he didn't want to brush against her but she didn't care if he did.

She had four elder brothers. They fought all the time. He had sisters; they never fought.

'Move,' he said through gritted teeth.

'Make me,' she said cheerfully.

He stopped, thought for a moment, rubbing the top of his head briskly. She knew he did that when he was irritated or troubled. 'Very well,' he said at last. 'You can come swim too. But no splashing water on me.'

She grinned widely. 'Thank you, Vishnu Gupta!'

She darted forward and quickly planted a kiss on top of his head.

'Why did you *do* that?' he said, upset. He bent down sideways, trying to bring the end of his dhoti up to wipe his head. 'You always do that!'

She laughed and ran ahead of him on the path. 'Last one in is a stupid donkey!'

He dropped his dhoti and began sprinting as fast as he could run.

They leaped off the ledge and hit the water together.

The instant she came up, she began splashing water on him.

'Hey!' he shouted, 'I told you no splashing!'

'I'm washing your head,' she said cheekily, 'you wanted it clean, didn't you?' She raised one fist mischievously, 'I can scrub it clean for you too!'

He splashed back at her. 'Stay away from me!'

Much splashing ensued.

Finally, exhausted, they floated, arms and legs sprawled. The afternoon was warm, the sun was shining, but the creek water was cool and refreshing. Flowers were blooming in the trees on either side, birds chirped and twittered, and a fawn and her mother came to drink thirstily. The fawn paused to gaze at the strange two-legged animals in the water till her mother nudged her. She drank her fill before daintily skipping up the bank and into the woods again. It was one of those idyllic afternoons when time stood still and all seemed right with the world.

'What are you thinking about, Vishnu Gupta?' Vaishali asked suddenly.

'I'm thinking about whether Indra really came down to aid Raja Sudas defeat the 10 kings, or only sent his vajra to help flood the river Parusni.'

A splash of water covered his face, water going up his nose and into his open mouth. Vishnu lost his balance, splashed briefly, then paddled water as he turned to stare at her. 'Why did you do that?'

'I don't want to keep talking about the Rig Veda,' she said. 'You always talk about the Vedas or Vedangas, or the Upanishads or one of the scriptures.'

'What's wrong with that?'

'It reminds me of my father. Always giving examples from one of the scriptures. So-and-so is like Ravana in Lanka. Such-and-such is like Shalya at Kurukshetra. I'm fed up of always hearing scriptures. I hear all about it from my father at home.'

'What else is there to talk about?'

'Stuff, silly. People. Things. Places. Like did you hear that Ekaparnika is getting married to Samudranarayana from our neighbouring village?'

'Why would I care about that?' he asked scornfully. 'Marriages are silly.'

'You'll get married too, one day, won't you?' she said. 'Will you be silly too then?'

'I'll never get married,' he said, with the unshakeable confidence of a seven-year-old boy.

She laughed. 'Everybody gets married, silly. Otherwise you can't have children of your own.'

'I'll never have children,' he said, even more resolutely.

'If you never have children, then you'll have nobody to carry on your family line, and to inherit all the knowledge you acquire in your lifetime,' she said, still floating on her back and using her left hand to keep herself afloat. 'My father says not having children is the same as never having been born.'

'I don't care,' he said. He tried to paddle with only his left hand too, but water went up his nose and he sputtered and lost his balance again.

'Elbows and knees bent,' she said. 'Here, let me show you.'

She made a move toward him, but he splashed away. 'No touching. You promised!'

'Why?' she asked irritably, 'am I an untouchable?'

'You're a girl,' he said.

'And you're a boy,' she said. 'So what? I know all about boys. I have four brothers, remember?'

He paddled farther away from her. 'I'm not your brother.'

She grinned impishly at him. 'I know! You're so sweet and silly. That's why I like playing with you. Not like my brothers, bullying and fighting all the time.'

A strange look came over her face.

'What?' he asked suspiciously.

'I was just thinking,' she said. 'Maybe when we get a little older, our parents could marry us.'

'WHAT?' he yelled, losing his balance and disappearing completely into the water. He came up, spluttering and spitting out water, paddling with all four limbs like a puppy learning to swim. 'That's impossible!'

'It's not, actually,' Vaishali said thoughtfully. 'Our fathers are the senior most brahmins in the village and....'

'Shut up!' he shouted, splashing water on her.

She giggled and splashed water back on him. She was much more efficient at it than he was.

After both had had their fill of splashing and shouting, they lay on the bank, getting their breath back.

She started to say something and his hand shot out in warning.

'No!' he said.

'How do you even know what I'm going to say?' she asked pleasantly.

'I don't want to hear anything you say,' he said, 'you talk all rubbish.'

'Nonsense,' she said. 'You're the one always talking about things that have nothing to do with us. I only talk sensible, normal things. Anyway, I was only going to say that my mother and I are going to be making pedas tomorrow. You like pedas, don't you?'

'I do,' he admitted. He was hungry and the mention of pedas had reminded him of the fact. He licked his lips, thinking of pedas.

'I'll make some especially for you, with extra jaggery, the way you like them.'

'And roasted mawa?'

'Extra roasted, for you,' she said. 'Till the mawa turns fully brown.'

Vishnu licked his lips again. 'I like pedas,' he said.

'I'll bring some for you if you meet me here again, by the creek.'

'Very well,' he said.

She jumped to her feet.

'Where are you going?' he asked, surprised.

'Home, silly. Where else? I still have to pick up the firewood I collected and take it home.' She stopped and frowned. 'I was supposed to make two trips because we need more so we can make the pedas tomorrow, but it's already getting late.'

He thought for a moment then stood up. 'I'll help you carry it. That way you'll have two bundles and we'll only need one trip.'

'Let's go,' she said, and started to run up the path. 'Last one has to carry the heavier bundle!'

He ran after her.

∽

He ate the last of the pedas with his eyes closed, face raised to the clear blue afternoon sky. 'Swarga,' he said in a reverential tone. 'Swarga.'

'I knew you would like them better this time,' Vaishali said, happily. She dusted off the crumbs and tucked away the empty cloth in which she had carried the pedas. 'I took special care.'

He opened his eyes at last, smacking his lips and licking his fingertips. 'Are they all finished?' he asked, disappointed.

'I can bring more tomorrow,' she said.

His face brightened. Then it fell again.

'What happened?' she asked.

'I can't come tomorrow,' he said.

Now, she was disappointed. 'Why not?'

'We're leaving.'

Her eyes widened. She sat up straight, startled. 'What? Who's leaving?'

'My whole family. All of us.'

'What do you mean, leaving? Where are you going?'

'To Pataliputra.'

'The capital?' she asked. 'To the Magadha Empire? Whatever for?'

He shrugged. 'My father wants to attend some big conference of brahmins.'

'So why are all of you going?'

'My mother has always wanted to visit the big city. She has a cousin there. So we'll have a place to stay. And naturally, my sisters and I aren't going to stay here alone. Though I don't know why. I'm perfectly capable of staying on my own and taking care of myself.'

Vaishali laughed. 'You? Vishnu Gupta, you can't tie your own dhoti without your mother's help!'

'Rubbish!' he said, indignant, 'I can tie my own dhoti perfectly well on my own!'

'And what will you eat while your mother is gone? Pedas?'

At the mention of pedas, he turned wistful again. 'I wish I could. Maybe I could eat at your house. After all, you are brahmins too.'

Then he shook his head. 'But we have to go. I want to hear my father speak at the conference too. And I want to attend the conference. My father says I will hear many interesting interpretations and discussions there. It will be good for my education. Besides, the truth is, there's nobody here in Chanak to talk to about anything interesting.'

She folded her hands and glared at him. 'Nobody?'

'Well, nobody interested in knowledge and scriptures,' he added, 'you know what I mean.'

'And there'll be nobody there in Pataliputra to give you my special pedas,' she said irritably. Then she softened. 'When will you be back?'

'I'm not sure. Probably a few days?'

'Silly! It takes at least a week just to reach Pataliputra on foot. Even on horseback it takes days.'

'Oh, in that case, weeks, I supposed. Maybe months. My mother says she hasn't seen her cousin in years.'

At the mention of weeks, months and years, Vaishali's face fell. 'Well,' she said, then fell silent.

They sat together, not saying anything. The day wore on slowly.

Across the creek, on the far bank, a lioness slunk out of the trees and crouched at the water's edge, lapping to her heart's content. Her yellow eyes stayed on the humans across the water, watching them intently. When she was done, she smacked her chops, washing off the excess water, and eyed Vishnu for a long moment. He swallowed nervously, suddenly wondering if he could run faster than a lion could swim. He glanced sideways at Vaishali to see if she was looking at the lioness too, but she was frowning down at the mud, a strange expression on her face.

'Why are you making that funny face?' he asked.

She turned away from him suddenly.

'Vaishali?' he asked.

She sat hunched over, her back to him for a moment. He saw her shoulders shake once. He thought she must be laughing. He glimpsed movement out the corner of his eye and turned to look at the spot where the lioness had been crouched. But the lioness was gone, vanished back into the darkness of the grove as silently as she had appeared. Vishnu breathed a sigh of relief.

∽

'Vishnu! Vishnu!'

All heads turned to look back. They were already on the dirt road leading out of the village, Vishnu's father in the lead, with his mother and sisters behind. Vishnu had a stick resting on his shoulder, his lota and belongings tied up tightly at the end.

He turned and saw Vaishali sprinting toward him.

'I went to your house,' she said as she reached them. 'I saw you were already gone.'

Vishnu Gupta's sisters were whispering. He glanced at them sideways, frowning. 'What is it?' he said curtly to Vaishali.

She thrust a bundle at him. 'I wanted to give you this.' She came up next to him and whispered into his ear. 'Pedas!'

He grinned, happy.

Vaishali darted in and gave him a quick kiss on the top of his bald head.

His sisters laughed.

He scowled.

'Hey!' he said.

Vaishali darted back. 'Safe travels!'

He used the bundle of pedas to try and wipe the top of his head.

His sisters were giggling when he turned to glare at them. 'Shut up!' he said.

His mother and father glanced at each other and smiled a mysterious grown-up smile, then turned and continued walking.

Vishnu walked behind them.

After a moment, he turned and stole a glance in the direction of the village.

Vaishali was running back, her bare feet kicking up dust as she went.

He smelled the pedas and his mouth watered. He grinned to himself and followed his family on the road to Pataliputra.

4

Rakshasa.

He liked the nickname they had given him.

It was spoken in his absence, spoken in hushed voices in private rooms, whispered into ears of powerful people. But he had learned about it anyway. He had spasas everywhere, and they told him everything. From time to time, he rotated them—had them arrested, beaten, and tortured till they revealed everything they knew, relevant or not—just to be sure they were still loyal to him. Of course, the ones he rotated out of his spy network were useless afterwards, mindless shivering hulks of human beings incapable of even the most basic human tasks; most died or killed themselves soon after release. They served as warnings to the active spasas. What the fools didn't know was that this was the fate that lay in wait for *all* his spies eventually; he only let them believe that their service would be rewarded with wealth, promotions or courtiership, among other things.

The truth was, once a person worked as a spy for Rakshasa, he was no good for anything else. They knew too much to be allowed to remain at large. So he rotated them in, replacing them with an ever-flowing supply of new arrivals.

He stood at the verandah of his palatial apartments on the highest level of Pataligrama Fort. All of Pataliputra lay sprawled before him, naked and helpless before the lust of his ambitions. From here he could see all access points into the capital city of the Magadha Empire. The Fort itself was the most heavily armed and defensible structure in the vast, bustling city. Even the Imperial Palace where Emperor Mahapadma Nanda and his family resided, while glorious and lavish in its luxury, was vulnerable if the Imperial Guard was not there to defend it.

Rakshasa did not trust human beings alone to protect his life; he needed to feel the hard, dense, solid structure of stone around himself to feel safe. People could be bought, persuaded, corrupted. Stone remained stone. He patted the balustrade of the verandah, appreciating the solidity of its construction. He had tunnels beneath the fort, secret doorways everywhere, food and wealth stored to last him for years if besieged or forced to flee. In his 30-plus years alive, he had been exposed to every form of human betrayal imaginable—and been responsible for more than any one man's share of such betrayals himself.

Rakshasa trusted no one, was friends with no one, loved and was loved by no one. It was the way he wanted it.

It was why he was nicknamed Rakshasa.

His given birth name was Kartikeya, after the indomitable son of Shiva and Parvati. He had disliked the name almost as much as he had disliked his parents and family. Over the years, as he rose from a simple brahmin in the service of the Shishunaga Emperors, to an Amatya, ministering advice and knowledge to the dynasty, he had learned that goodness was overrated. Cruelty, despotism, tyranny; these were the things people feared. And what people feared, they respected. Goodness, kindness, gentleness, righteousness, these were all noble sentiments of dharma for the soft, weak and poor. Real power lay in the hands of the oppressors, those who took what they desired, by force, violently and brutally, without compunction or mercy. A man who raised a pet dog kindly received only licks and woofs in response. A man who beat and starved his pet dog created a vicious guard, one who would kill on sight in return for his day's rations.

The Kartikeyas of the world earned admiration, honour, glory.

It took a Rakshasa to govern, to rule, to control.

He watched the ebb and flow of the network of rivers of humanity below, streaming into the gates of the city, moving through the streets, engaged in the everyday business of buying and selling everything that was possible to buy and sell. It made him feel powerful. The knowledge that every single trade or exchange of coin that was being transacted earned him more wealth pleased him.

True, the majority of the tax collected on all transactions went to the Imperial coffers, but in order to be permitted to transact, all those merchants, sellers and traders, had to pay him a percentage as well, on top of the Imperial Taxes. This unofficial levy was collected by his network of Cutters, hard-muscled cold-hearted brutes who ensured that Rakshasa received a cut of every business transaction conducted in the capital. This included the black economy; the omni-present web of illegal, criminal and unauthorised business that went on in the back alleys, dark corners, and locked rooms where every manner of appetite could be indulged for a price. Murder-for-hire, prostitution, illegal gambling, and an astonishing variety of other activities fed the darker tastes of the citizenry as well as the nobility from the mansions and lavish estates of the Upper City, separated from the Lower City by an unsurmountable wall.

Rakshasa glanced up to his left, gazing at the hill upon which the Upper City stood. The large estates, vast manicured gardens, and much less crowded, tree-lined avenues and boulevards were evidence of the great wealth of the ancient families that held the maximum influence in the Empire.

He allowed himself a sneering smile. Let those rich fools believe they held all the reins of power and wealth. They were nothing without the protection of the Emperor, and the Emperor listened to him, Maha-amatya Rakshasa. If he chose, he could have every last one of the members of those great Houses slaughtered in their sleep. But he needed them too, just as he needed the common citizenry haggling and squabbling in the crowded filthy streets below. It was in his interests for the ordinary business of commerce and politics to continue, for Pataliputra to grow and prosper. The more it grew, the bigger the Cut he would earn.

But Rakshasa was also starting to get restless.

He wanted more than just a Cut. A sliver, really, since the Emperor was the one who took the biggest Cut in the name of taxes.

Rakshasa wanted a slice, maybe even a chunk of flesh, taken from the choicest portions of the naked body of Pataliputra. Enough to bring him on par with those nose-in-the-air families up on the hill in their marbled mansions. Enough to buy him an army. To make him an Emperor in his own right.

He had no intention of actually becoming Emperor. Make no mistake about it. He was a brahmin and was content to remain at the side of the raj-kshatriyas that sat upon the throne. They were warriors, and warriors went to war, as their varna demanded. Sooner or later, they fought and died, or, more often than not, were killed and replaced. They were mere pieces in the great game of chaupat that was politics.

It was the brahmin by the side of the king that had the real power. The Maha-amatya beside the Emperor. Rakshasa by the side of Mahapadma Nanda. He was the kingmaker—or more accurately, the Emperor-Maker. He had *made* Mahapadma Nanda emperor, replacing not just his predecessor, Rakshasa's own former lord, but his entire dynasty. That was true power.

What he needed to go with that power was wealth. No matter how much he connived, schemed and manipulated, even skimming a healthy fraction of the imperial taxes, his growing fortune was no comparison to the ancestral wealth of those High Houses, and their wealth in turn was no comparison to that of the Imperial Coffers.

Rakshasa wanted it all. All the wealth in the world. He believed in abundance, that the universe existed to serve him, and that he was owed all it had to give him. If it chose not to give willingly, he was happy to reach out and snatch.

This seemingly small-scale Cutting had made him rich, but not rich enough.

The question was how to make him the richest of all. Richer than the Emperor himself, without actually becoming Emperor himself.

That was the conundrum that occupied Rakshasa's thoughts of late.

∽

'Maha-amatyaji.'

Rakshasa turned to see his aide standing across the large room, head bowed deferentially, hands joined before him. As he had been trained. As all Rakshasa's aides had been trained. Training was very simple: have those who did not greet him appropriately executed. Everyone else learned instantly. He didn't know the aide's name, though he assumed he had one. He had over 50 of them, each serving a function, often overlapping with others, to better enable Rakshasa to oversee everyone's performance, and to enable him to filter out all but those powerful and wealthy enough to earn the right to an audience with the most powerful man in the Magadha Empire. This man being himself, the true power behind the Imperial Throne.

'Speak,' he said now to the aide.

The aide took a few steps forward into the room, keeping his eyes and head lowered and palms joined. 'The Emperor has expressed a desire to seek your valuable advice, when it pleases you to attend him at court.'

A flicker of movement caught Rakshasa's eye. He was still standing at the balustrade, looking out over the city. *His* city. He glanced down, his eyes seeking out and finding what had attracted his attention. It was a boy, just one of the countless youth wandering the streets of Pataliputra, seeking work or on some errand or mission. Except that this one wasn't seeking work, he was at work. Rakshasa watched as the boy brushed past a pair of rich traders looking at silks at a merchant's stall. The boy was very quick and skilled, but Rakshasa's eyes were quicker, his skills sharper, and he saw the deft movements with which the boy cut loose the purses of all three merchants and moved the hefty pouches into a secret pocket inside his own clothing. It was neatly done, smoother and quicker than most of his ilk. Rakshasa employed a few common cut-pockets and cut-throats as well, in keeping with his philosophy that anything that made money was worth taking a cut of. He had watched them at work and knew the tricks of the trade fairly well. He was impressed by the youth's skills.

'There is a youth in a bearskin coat working Silk Market, cutting pockets,' Rakshasa said to his aide, who was still waiting with bowed head and joined palms. 'Have him brought up to me.' He added: 'Alive and unharmed.' An earlier aide had delivered a person he had wanted with his throat cut and body covered with bruises, rendering the person of no use to him. He had ordered his guards to do the same to the aide, which had served as a lesson to all his aides. But, since then, he had begun clarifying his orders.

'At once, Maha-amatya.' The aide spoke quickly to *his* aide, standing just outside the door, and the aide's aide scurried away to have the order carried out. Rakshasa liked multiple levels and layers of personnel. It provided structure. People needed structure. It made them aware that there was a hierarchy, and of their own place in that hierarchy.

The aide was still waiting.

Rakshasa let him wait. He knew that if the aide had brought him the Emperor's request, it had been conveyed by one of the Emperor's own envoys, and by keeping his own aide waiting, Rakshasa was also keeping the Emperor's envoy waiting. It pleased him to do so, because in Rakshasa's Pataliputra one of the measures of the stature of a person was the length of time they kept you waiting. The Shishunagas had been masters of this fine art: From time to time when a person of great influence was found to be offensive to the Emperor and sentenced to death for the offense, the Emperor would invariably receive urgent pleas for mercy from the powerful family. Rather than reject the plea and offend that family in turn, Shishunaga would receive the plea with due respect and pretend to consider it seriously, then continue to consider it until the time of execution had passed, and the unfortunate offender had been parted from his or her head. At that time, Shishunaga would pardon the offender, thereby restoring honour to the powerful family, but it would of course be too late for the executed individual, which maintained the honour of Shishunaga himself.

After a few moments, there was a commotion and two Imperial Guards entered, each holding an arm of the youth Rakshasa had spotted at work from his verandah. The boy was protesting and struggling despite the impossibility of escaping his muscular captors.

'You are making a mistake! I am not the person you are seeking. I bought this coat off a Gandahari merchant on the Uttarapatha. It belonged to someone else before me. He's probably the one you want.'

One of the guards thumped the youth on his head to shut him up; both of them then forced the boy to his knees.

The aide stepped forward again. 'Maha-amatya, the youth you requested.'

At the mention of the words "Maha-amatya", the youth's eyes widened. Rakshasa took pleasure in seeing the impact his title alone had upon the boy. All the bluster and denial went out of the fellow at once; he stopped struggling, and dropped his head and clasped his hands together in a gesture of supplication.'Maha-amatya! Forgive me. I did not know I was being brought into your own august presence.'

Rakshasa gestured to the guards. 'Strip him.'

The guards began to yank off the boy's black bear coat. He complied with them, stripping the rest of his clothes off. There were a surprising number of layers for a mildly cool spring day. Even the guards blinked as he peeled off layer after layer. Finally, a heap lay on the floor at his feet, and the youth himself, a skinny boy not even half as broad and well-fed as he had seemed under all those layers, knelt before Rakshasa, hands joined and head lowered.

'Tell the boy to show me the purses he stole,' Rakshasa commanded his aide. He knew better than to address the youth directly; that often gave the person the impression that he could address Rakshasa directly.

The youth scrambled through the garments, pulling out purse after purse from pocket after pocket. The aide and the guards stared at the growing heap of purses on the floor.

'Ask him to also show me the other valuables he took. Show me everything.'

The boy complied without needing to be prodded. He removed a small cache of rings, amulets, bracelets, waist-chains and necklaces. Rakshasa used a longstaff to prod the collection of purses and jewellery.

'Not bad for a cut-pocket,' he said to his aide. 'Now ask him who his fence is in the city.'

For the first time, the boy did not respond on his own. Even though the youth had already spoken in Pali, the aide repeated the instruction in Prakrit and common dialects as well. The youth glanced up hesitantly, a lock of his hair falling over his brow, almost concealing his scared eyes.

'Maha-amatya,' he began.

He was rewarded by a thump on the back from one of the guards. 'Speak only to the Maha-amatya's aide,' the guard said, 'or you will have your tongue cut off.'

'My lord,' the youth said uncertainly, 'I am new to Pataliputra City. I arrived only a few days earlier. I have not yet made any friends or connections. I was still seeking out suitable contacts who might be interested in purchasing such items as I might have to offer for sale.'

The aide conveyed the gist of this to his master.

Rakshasa was amused. 'It takes some insolence for a stranger to saunter into my city and to start cutting pockets without so much as a Namaskara to me.'

The youth kept his head lowered but Rakshasa saw the boy's eyes flicker from side to side in panic.

'Where did he learn to cut?' Rakshasa asked his aide.

The boy named several smaller cities and towns. Rakshasa was impressed. Most cut-pockets tended to stick to one place, thinking that they knew the place, the streets, and the people well enough to feed off them at their leisure; this was a strength at first, but eventually it was also their failing. Sooner or later, even the most lax town authorities grew wise to such cutters and cracked down on them. It was one thing to move through a crowded marketplace cutting pockets and purses when people were distracted, but if someone kept a sharp lookout for your antics, sooner or later they would get lucky and spot you. Most cut-pockets were caught this way, but by the time they were apprehended, it was too late for them to learn from their mistake. The penalty for cutting pockets was the same as the penalty for almost any crime in Magadha: execution on the spot. A dead cut-pocket couldn't learn from their mistakes and other cut-pockets always assumed they had been caught because they weren't slick enough. That was another failing of the species: ego. Rakshasa had yet to meet a modest cut-pocket.

The boy was trembling by this time. Beads of sweat had appeared on his upper lip where he had only recently begun to grow a little fuzz. Too young to pass for a man; too old to suit the tastes of the High Nobles who favoured boys. He was pretty enough, but Rakshasa had better uses in mind for him than the Lower City brothels. Any pretty boy could be a prostitute; a pretty boy with this one's talent could do far more.

'Leave us,' Rakshasa said suddenly.

His aide was startled. The guards obeyed without question, exiting at once. The aide hesitated a moment, then withdrew with a deeper bow, palms still joined together obsequiously.

Rakshasa used his stick to poke through the small cache on the floor, then turned his attention to the bear coat.

'Stay silent and listen,' he said.

The boy quivered as if he had been expecting a death sentence, but bowed his head lower and kept silent. He was sweating openly now despite the cool spring air wafting in from the open verandah and windows. Rakshasa liked to dress warm and keep his doors and windows open, unlike most imperials and nobles who seemed to love staying in windowless chambers, no doubt the better to keep their activities private. Rakshasa had no need of privacy. Everyone knew what he was and what he did and he flaunted his worst excesses: that was his way of showing his power to the world. He was Rakshasa after all, and as a mythical blood-slurping demon he might as well live up to his reputation.

'From time to time I have need of boys with certain talents, to perform certain tasks for me. When I have need of your services, I will send word to you. You will carry out your instructions to the letter. Failure to obey will result in suffering and death. Any attempt to flee the city will result in capture, suffering and death. You may continue to ply your trade, but the city is divided up into sectors and each sector is allocated to my own cutters, and the allocations change periodically, to avoid recognition. You will be allotted a sector and informed of the change of allocations through the usual cutter network. Six-tenths of everything you cut will be paid as protection to my representatives. If you attempt to conceal any part of your takings, it will result in suffering and death. If you steal from or cut another Cutter, it will result in suffering and death. Any attempt to enter any other line of criminal activity will result in suffering and death. Nod once if you are clear on all these points.'

The brown-haired head bobbed once enthusiastically.

'Take your garments, but leave all the cuttings. Leave my presence now and never return unless specifically called for. You will dress now.'

The boy scrambled to snatch his several layers of garments,

clutching them in his arms and moving toward the door with the creeping movements of a roach on the verge of slipping into concealment, away from human eyes.

'One moment,' Rakshasa said.

The boy froze.

'By what name are you known? Speak it once and depart immediately. Do not turn around.'

'Chandra,' the boy said, and scurried out of the room.

After a moment the aide returned again.

Rakshasa gestured at the purses and jewellery on the floor.

'Add these to my cuttings, and find me the Cutter allocated to the Silk Market.'

The aide bowed in acknowledgement. 'I shall have him brought here at once.'

'Don't bring him here,' Rakshasa snapped. 'Have him taken to the kosaghar.'

At the mention of the kosaghar, the aide's hands trembled. The kosaghar in most houses referred to a crying room, an empty chamber where family members sat in silence after a loved one's death, to grieve in private. In Maha-amatya Rakshasa's house, it meant a number of underground dungeons where anyone who displeased him was taken to be interrogated, tortured, or executed. Nobody who went into his kosaghar ever returned alive. People had been known to kill themselves rather than be taken to Rakshasa's kosaghar. The aide knew what the order meant.

'And you may send word back to his Imperial Highness that I will attend him shortly.'

Rakshasa flicked his hand to dismiss the aide, who scurried away almost as desperately as the cut-pocket.

5

A short while later, Maha-amatya Rakshasa entered the palace complex, his tall black-clad figure terminating conversations and causing eyes to widen, be averted, or to drop downwards at once. He did not stop to exchange greetings with any of the High Nobles or visiting royalty he passed along the way; he was not a diplomat or a courtier. Everyone knew better than to attempt to greet or interrupt his progress. They were content simply to let him pass before heaving a silent or overt sigh of relief and resuming their interrupted activity.

The opulence of the Imperial Court did not impress Maha-amatya, nor did the vulgar displays of grandeur in the architecture, art and furnishings, the scantily clad entertainers, or the familiar white and black faces of foreign ambassadors currently being hosted by the Emperor. Rakshasa considered all art, entertainment and social niceties to be a waste of energy and time. To him, the creation of wealth and amassing of power were all that mattered, and in his opinion, every waking moment of the Emperor ought to be spent solely occupied in those pursuits. The vulgar displays of flesh, food and wine disgusted him. He was a strict vegetarian as his brahmanical varna demanded, though the fact was that few brahmins in high places adhered to those restrictions, especially in private.

To him, even the massive amounts of food, fruit and sweets of every description were gluttonous excess. His disapproval of all these indulgences was plainly visible on his long bony features; he made no attempt to conceal it.

'Maha-amatya Kartikeya,' the Emperor said as he approached the imperial dais. 'How good of you to come to see us.'

Rakshasa bowed his head at the appropriate angle, not a degree too low or too high. He straightened himself immediately. 'How may I be of service to your Imperial Highness?' he asked in a suitably polite tone.

Mahapadma Nanda chuckled, drinking from the jewelled goblet that an attendant held up to his lips, then accepting a peeled grape that another attendant offered his thick lips. 'I would ask you to join me and my distinguished foreign visitors in some drinking and dining, as one would usually expect of most Prime Ministers.' He raised his voice to include the foreigners seated around. 'But our Prime Minister is quite an unusual person. He has no indulgences.'

The visitors exclaimed as their interpreters communicated this news, and then turned to gaze at Rakshasa as though examining a new species found in the deep jungle.

'All my energies are invested into the continued expansion, prosperity and security of Magadha, your Highness,' Rakshasa said, bowing his head slightly again. 'I live to serve.'

Mahapadma chuckled again. He had a tiny speck of food in his chin-beard. An attendant cleaned it with a silk napkin embroidered with gold. 'Yes, yes, we know you work incessantly. It's boring but necessary work,' he explained to his audience, who nodded in agreement, glancing sympathetically at Rakshasa, commiserating with a fellow servant of the Empire. Rakshasa had no doubt that each of them served rulers back in their distant kingdoms who would like nothing better than to have him stretched out on a rack, his already long limbs elongated even further to force him to divulge the secrets of how one went about building an empire in this vast, abundant and richly resourceful sub-continent. The smiling interpreters who stood behind each visiting dignitary's chair were also tasters, responsible for tasting each and every item the dignitaries consumed to ensure they weren't being poisoned. Mahapadma himself had several tasters, each an expert in various poisons and combinations; he needed that many because of the high mortality rate. The Emperor lost at least one poison-taster each week, often as many as three in some weeks.

Rakshasa would rather sit to dinner with a nest of cobras than dine with this group of smiling foreigners, each ready to murder everyone else if it would further their interests in even the smallest way.

Talk of Rakshasa's eating habits prompted a speech by Mahapadma on the eating habits of his people. He droned on for a while about spices and their respective health-affirming properties.

Rakshasa waited for the Emperor to get to the point. He was accustomed to Mahapadma's rambling. It was one of the minor privileges of being an emperor. Rakshasa took his satisfaction from the time he took to respond to Mahapadma's summons, while Mahapadma took his pleasure from making these little monologues while Rakshasa stood, waiting patiently.

Finally, he came to the business of the hour.

'Ah, Maha-amatya,' he said, as if only now remembering that the Prime Minister had been standing patiently before him for the better part of an hour. 'I have a quandary to discuss with you. Perhaps talking it over with you may help clear my thinking.'

Rakshasa made no comment. He knew as well as the Emperor did that Mahapadma could not think his way out of a quandary if his life depended on it. All he cared about was his body's needs and cravings, and how to satisfy them in the most interesting and entertaining manner possible. If he wanted to maintain the illusion of a conference, Rakshasa would play along—and afterward, he would do whatever thinking was needed to solve the Emperor's current predicament. In many ways, he was a midwife to the Empire, cleaning up the Emperor's messes just as a wet-nurse would clean up a baby's leavings. This caused him no great distress; it was what he did. Mahapadma's very dependency on him for such things was what made his position so secure. Without him, not only Mahapadma's Empire, but his entire daily existence would fall apart.

'I remain at your service, Imperial Highness,' Rakshasa said.

'Yes, yes,' Mahapadma said absently, 'it would be rude of me to leave my honoured visitors now. Perhaps we shall reconvene later after I am done dining with them? Yes. Later would be best. I shall send for you at the appropriate time.'

Rakshasa inclined his head, not needing to state the obvious: that Mahapadma could simply have sent him a message saying that he would be needed later in the day, instead of summoning him urgently and making him wait all this time while he lectured these half-drunk foreigners about the wondrous properties of spices. 'As you wish, Highness,' he said, and began to retreat.

'Oh, and by the way, since you are here anyway, do look in on Dhana Nanda, will you? I believe he has a little matter he requires assistance resolving.'

The Emperor resumed his conversation with the foreign dignitaries.

Rakshasa completed his exit and left the court. He understood now why Mahapadma had summoned him urgently as well as why he had pretended to want his advice on the 'quandary'. He knew now that there was no quandary at all. There would be no discussion later in the day, or if there was one, it would not be about matters of empire.

The real reason Rakshasa had been summoned was to deal with the matter concerning Prince Dhana Nanda. The Emperor had not wanted to reveal this openly and had deliberately created this facade to deflect attention from the real problem. It was nicely done. After all, he had had a good teacher: Rakshasa himself had indoctrinated Mahapadma in these subterfuges and methods. The word 'matter' was the key: it was Mahapadma's way of letting him know that whatever shenanigan Dhana Nanda had been up to this time, it was serious.

As he strode briskly through the palace complex, heading for the princely palaces, Rakshasa mused on what it might be. It was always serious where Dhana Nanda was concerned. The eldest son of the Emperor was not just spoiled rotten. All children of emperors and kings were spoiled rotten. The simple fact of being born into their privileged position, the security and isolation that came with it, the sheer quantum of wealth, luxury, power and subservience that they were accustomed to from birth made them incapable of comprehending the realities of existence outside the Imperial Palace. They were like Gods living in their own private lokas, situated on some heavenly, other-dimensional plane. If everyone around you treated you like a god, worshipped you like a god, served you as a god, and if you had god-like powers over people and places, it was impossible to fully accept that you were *not* a god. Especially since nobody around you would ever press home that point. If anything, they fed the delusion. Yes, yes, you are god. God-Emperor of Magadha, the greatest empire in the known world.

Nothing compares to your wealth, your power, your influence. You are supreme, above all others.

He passed the princely palaces of the other children of Mahapadma Nanda as well as the queens' palaces. Nobody greeted him or interrupted his progress. They were all occupied in their own private worlds of feasting, debauchery and indulgence. For his part, Rakshasa ignored everyone he encountered as well. He was on a task, and even greeting everyone he met would require hours of formality. Besides, his spies provided him with regular updates on every activity of everyone who mattered. He knew every vice and dirty habit of every last imperial family member.

Which was why he was surprised that he had not heard of Dhana Nanda's latest indiscretion, whatever it might be. After all, his spy had always fed him precise and prompt information of every previous incident. In several cases, he had even cleaned up the mess without informing Mahapadma. It was part of his job description to ensure the welfare of the imperial family, by any means necessary. But to have a serious incident, a 'matter' as the Emperor called it, without hearing anything about it for hours—that was unusual. He made a mental note to himself to have the spasa in question reprimanded for the lapse. And by reprimanded, he meant suffering and death, of course. It was the only way to ensure complete compliance from the replacement.

Yet it still bothered him as he finally approached the Crown Prince's lavish palace.

Why was I not informed?

He learned the reason a moment later.

The scene in Dhana Nanda's bedroom was straight out of Rakshasa's own kosaghar. There, it was commonplace to see this much blood splashed everywhere. But here, in a princely chamber, the sheer volume of plasma expended and spilled across every available surface of the chamber, on the floors, walls, even a few splashes on the ceiling, was something Rakshasa had not been expecting.

He started to count the bodies lying around and gave up after double digits. More than ten. Perhaps more than twenty. They were mostly young women he saw, but a few were young men too. He understood now why his spy had not sent him word of the Crown Prince's latest indiscretion: she herself was lying dead, sprawled across a couch, her naked body disfigured with gaping slashes.

The wounds appeared to have been inflicted with multiple weapons, all of which were still lying around as well. Some of them were still clutched in the hands of the naked bodies and from the positions and wounds, it did not take a genius of Rakshasa's level to see that a melee of some sort had taken place here. A score of beautiful young people, all stark naked, probably drunk judging from all the goblets and skins of wine also lying about, all hacking and slashing and stabbing each other to death. If it had been a party, it must have been the most fiendish party imaginable.

Rakshasa saw no sign of Dhana Nanda himself. That was as he had expected. Even with his spy dead, the Crown Prince's demise was not a piece of information that would have failed to reach his ears. The first in the line of succession, Dhana Nanda stood to inherit the entire Magadha Empire some day. That made him as important to Rakshasa as Mahapadma himself. Perhaps even more important.

He went into the innermost chamber, the sleeping room.

Dhana Nanda was on the bed, cradling something in his lap. He was dressed as usual in his princely robes, the luxurious silks and jewelled garments strangely adult on his little seven-year-old body. There was blood on his clothes, on his hands, his feet, his body, his face. He was bathed in blood, with only a few patches of bare skin or unstained garment showing. The blood had dried and congealed on him over the past few hours. From the state of the bodies in the outer chamber, Rakshasa had estimated that they would have been killed perhaps only a couple of hours earlier. Which meant that Mahapadma had sent for him at once.

Dhana Nanda looked up as Rakshasa towered over him. He had been crying, two lines of tear tracks cutting through the blood patches that stained his fat rosy cheeks.

'Mamatya,' he said, using the childish reduction that he used to say when he was too young to pronounce the Prime Minister's full title. 'Look.'

He held out the object that he had cradled in his lap. Rakshasa saw it was a little kitten, barely the size of his palm. It lay limply like a furry rag in the Crown Prince's little hands.

'Airavata is dead.'

Rakshasa looked down at the dead kitten. 'All things die, Dhana.'

Dhana looked up at him. 'I don't like dying. I don't want Airavata dead. I want him alive! Make him alive *now*! I command it!' He raised his voice with each sentence, reaching a shouting pitch by the end. His voice was hoarse, suggesting that he had done a fair bit of shouting earlier as well.

Rakshasa knew better than to argue. He had an inkling that even insisting on the impossibility of restoring a dead kitten to life might have been the cause of all the dead naked bodies lying in the outer room.

'Give him to me,' he said, holding out his hand.

Dhana Nanda stared up at him. 'You will make Airavata alive again?'

'I will,' Rakshasa said.

Dhana Nanda grinned, revealing several gaps in his lower teeth where his milk teeth had rotted away and new teeth not yet grown in their place. He was fond of sweets. He held up both hands, offering the dead kitten up like a sacrifice.

Rakshasa took the kitten, pretending to handle it gently, and turned to go. He paused.

'What happened to all the people?' he asked, looking back at the little prince sitting on his bed.

Dhana Nanda yawned. He was sleepy and probably exhausted from all the crying and shouting. Not to mention whatever other activities he had been involved in.

'They couldn't make Airavata alive again.'

Rakshasa waited but that was it. Dhana Nanda had nothing further to say. He saw the Crown Prince lean back against his pillows, his head lolling, eyes glazing over as he fell asleep almost instantly with the ease of the very young. Rakshasa decided that was a formal dismissal and left the chambers.

They couldn't make Airavata alive again. That was as good an explanation as any, he supposed. The body count was higher than he had seen, but a dead pet was something to get upset about, after all. It would upset any normal child. And since Dhana Nanda was not normal, it had upset him much more, causing him to vent his anger and frustration on his maids and servers, by ordering them to kill each other. Why the nakedness? Who knew? Perhaps Dhana Nanda had wanted them all to strip first, or to perform some lewd act for his entertainment. Perhaps he had wanted them to perform lewd acts *while* they killed each other. It didn't matter anymore. They were dead and it was a mess to be cleaned up, that was all.

He came out of the Crown Prince's chambers and found a long line of maids and servants and imperial guards all standing in a row, waiting for his instructions.

'Clean up all the mess in there,' he said, 'Get rid of the bodies the usual way.' Cremation was the usual way, but not with due rites and rituals—simply a mass cremation done at the rear of the palace complex, where all such 'messes' were disposed of as always. 'When the Crown Prince awakens, clean him up too. He is in need of a bath—but only after he wakes up.'

He saw a maid who looked slightly less stupid than the others and handed the dead kitten to her. As he dusted his hands by slapping his palms against each other, he said, 'Find me a kitten exactly like that, same colouring, same markings, same size. Give it to the crown prince with my compliments. Tell him, "Maha-amatya has made Airavata alive again. Here he is".' He looked at the girl. 'Do you understand?'

She dipped her head sharply.

He strode away without looking back. His work here was done.

6

Chandra saw the thieves following the brahmin family and knew they were going to do worse than rob them.

It was no concern of his; he was working the sector he had been allocated, and it was a good payday. A lot of outsiders were pouring into the city on account of some big intellectual conference and they were all brahmins, the majority of them from small towns and villages. Most of them weren't carrying anything worth stealing. Some literally owned only their copper lota and the simple clothes on their body. In his independent days, Chandra wouldn't have wasted his time working this bunch. It just wasn't worth the effort. But now he worked for The Man. And The Man expected his people to take everything that was there to take.

'Not your place to decide what's worth stealing or not, boss,' his sector head had drawled to him through a mouthful of chewing tobacco earlier, 'your job's to cut, so cut.' The man turned his head and spat a mouthful of brilliant red tobacco juice at his feet, splattering the footwear and bottom of the crisp white dhotis of a brahmin walking past. The priest was so engrossed in taking in the sights of the big city that he didn't even realise that his pristine dhoti was now spotted with blood-red stains. 'See that?' the sector leader said, jerking a thumb at the clueless brahmin, 'like deer in the woods. You could cut their throats and they wouldn't know it till they fell facedown.'

Chandra knew better than to argue the point. He had been cuffed upside the head too many times for asking too many questions before. It was easier to just do his work. He had cut his usual quota of pockets today and all he had to show for it was a small pile of iron and brass coins, a handful of copper ones—not a single silver or gold—and several rudraksh prayer bead necklaces. Taking the necklaces was pointless; they were worth almost nothing; but he had to take something. When he went to show the sector head his meagre cuts, the man had taken the prayer bead necklaces and tossed them into the ditch. He had weighed the coins, looking dissatisfied with the haul.

'Need more than this,' he said, his cheek full of a wad of tobacco. 'What else these fools have?'

'Nothing,' Chandra said.

The man glanced at the endless stream of brahmins drifting past on the crowded street. 'They all have those little water pot things.' He jerked his head sideways as a group passed by, all carrying sticks on their shoulders with lotas wrapped with red cloth hanging at the end of the sticks.

'Lotas,' Chandra said.

'What're they made of?'

Chandra shrugged. 'Copper, I guess.'

The man showed his teeth, stained blood red and with flecks of tobacco between his cracked teeth. 'Copper will do. Get as many as you can.'

Chandra hesitated.

The man was already counting the coins, separating the coppers from the cheaper ones. He glanced up sharply. 'Go on, then. Do your job. We got a quota to fill.'

'Those lotas,' he said, 'they're usually filled with Gangajal. Holy water they carry all the way from the sacred river.'

'So?'

'So...they'll be upset when they find them missing. The lota as well as the water.'

The sector leader glared at him. 'Toss the water, bring the lotas, as many as you can.' He paused, thinking, 'At least 20 by end of day.'

Chandra stared at him. 'Twenty!'

'Twenty-five then,' the man said, looking at Chandra with an expression that suggested he was happy to make it 30 or even more if Chandra had further objections.

Chandra raised his palms, giving up, and turned away. He cursed the man, the rest of the whole network and The Man. Not aloud. He would never make the mistake of ever speaking Maha-amatya's name or even his title aloud. One never knew who might be listening. During the nights when he sometimes rendezvoused with Cuts from other sectors, to exchange gossip and news, he had heard of the ones who made the mistake of resisting the system, trying to keep part of their Cut from their sector leaders, and on one occasion, about a Cut who had drunk too much honey wine and let slip a single word in his inebriated state. *Rakshasa*! Spoken with contempt. That was all it took. The next morning he was found floating face down in a cesspool.

He invested his energy into separating several brahmins from their lotas. He focused on the younger ones, especially the brahmacharyas who were in groups, trailing behind their white-bearded gurus. It wasn't hard. Many were visiting the city, *any* city, for the first time in their lives, and were all agog at the sights, sounds, smells. He would saunter behind a group as they wandered the winding streets of Lower City, slowed by their own curiosity as well as the dense crowds. Ingress into Pataliputra was designed in such a way that all visitors from the Uttarapada and Dakshinapada Gates had to traverse through a labyrinthine maze of crowded streets with stalls and vendors on both sides, constantly hawking goods, services, and trades. If you could resist spending your coin on one of the many savouries or enticing items—something that few visitors could manage—the Cuts would take your purse for you, relieving you of the pressure to shop!

City dwellers used short cuts through back alleys that cut through the heart of the maze. From Uttarapada Gate to the brahmin enclave, where all these brahmin visitors were headed, was actually a distance of barely a quarter of a mile. Five hundred steps at most. But because of the mercantile layout of the streets, it ended up being almost four times that distance, all full mile or even a mile and a half, depending on which route one took. And with tens of thousands of goggle-eyed brahmins and their brahmacharya acolytes thronging the streets, it could take a full hour just to cover even that short distance.

Chandra's sector was Uttara Market, the motley collection of vendors that began from the Uttarapada Gate and continued for about 300 square yards, every yard of which the visitors had to traverse, turning into a complex series of lefts and rights, essentially walking a grid pattern. Twenty streets and bylanes crisscrossing each other. Around 400 vendors and merchants clustered in that square block. And on a day like today, perhaps one or two thousand visitors, constantly streaming through.

This was one of the best and worst sectors to be a Cut in. Best, because the visitors had just come through the gate and were most distracted as they got their first view of the great metropolis and took in the sights, making them easy targets. Worst, because the vendors were all sellers of trinkets, snacks and minor low-value items, and few visitors stopped to spend much, wanting to explore more of the city before they got down to serious shopping. Mostly, people only stopped in Uttara Market to grab a quick bite, or to pick up a cheap trinket or two. Often, there were many wealthier visitors from the Northern provinces that came through the gate and they carried hefty purses as well as valuables. But not today. Today, it was a sea of white grinding past, with nothing but bald heads and lotas.

Chandra trawled lazily behind the group of brahmacharyas, pretending to gape at the stalls and colourful displays on either side with the same slack-jawed fascination that he saw on so many visitor's faces, while he gathered his quota of lotas. Quota of lotas! There was a phrase he had never thought he would ever be saying.

He had to keep taking breaks to deliver his collections to the sector leader. The lotas were bulky and made his overclothes bulge and clank oddly, drawing strange looks. He could manage to stuff a half dozen at a time and then he would have to break away to take a short cut through alleyways so narrow that only a slender man—or a young boy—could walk through easily, to Arka, the cheap liquor store outside which the sector leader and his goons sat all day. Chandra knew the man's name but preferred to think of him as Somatose, because the man started drinking by the time the sun crossed the mid-day peak, guzzled soma all day and invariably drank himself comatose by sundown.

He set down his latest haul of lotas on the rickety wooden plank that served as a table before which Somatose sat with legs sprawled. 'That makes 26 so far.'

Somatose chewed his tobacco plug, not bothering to even look at the little copper open-mouthed pots. 'These are worth crap. Get me something worth something.'

Chandra took in a deep breath and exhaled slowly before replying. 'You said to collect 25 lotas. I did.'

Somatose elbowed the lotas out of the way, scattering them across the plank. One clattered to the ground. 'All the Cuts are bringing in only lotas. Word from the top is no more lotas. Worth nothing.'

'They can be melted down to make copper coins,' Chandra said.

Somatose squinted up at him. It was nearing noon and the sun was almost overhead. 'You giving me an argument, boy?'

'No, sir.'

'Then go bring me something worth more than a few coppers. That's the order from on top.'

On top meant the Maha-amatya's mansion, the highest point in Lower City, looking down over the whole sprawled mess like a leopard on a tree top surveying a field full of buffaloes. Except the buffaloes were skinny and sparse today.

Chandra knew better than to argue further with Somatose. He had seen one of his fellow Cuts beaten down by the leader and his goons once; it had been enough to convince him that obedience was the only option.

He picked up a small purse from a merchant who had stopped to sample fried snacks at a food stall. The merchant looked wealthy but had clearly left his main purse elsewhere, probably buried in the large bundle of belongings carried by his weary servant. The small travel purse only contained a few coppers and one silver, but it was better than nothing.

Chandra was shadowing a trio of priests from Chinn, their long drooping moustaches and pigtails almost as distinctive as their far eastern features, when he saw the brahmin family.

The father walked in front, a serious scholarly looking fellow; one of those intent enough on his own thoughts to not care much about the attractions of the big city. He was squinting at nothing in particular with the look of a man deeply pondering some philosophical conundrum. The mother was holding the hands of her two younger daughters, both clearly first-time city visitors staring up round-eyed at the colourful trinkets dangling from the stall displays. The eldest daughter was walking behind the mother and sisters, holding onto the hand of the only son, a small brahmin boy with a face and eyes that shone with an interesting combination of intelligence and mischief. There were other brahmins who brought their families to the conference, but few had three daughters, and none had one as pretty as the eldest daughter of this family. Apart from her attractive looks, she also had a way of walking, holding her chin up that bore a strong family resemblance to her mother and her brother. Chandra was of the age when girls had begun to look more attractive than food and money. Well, *almost* as attractive as food. He took one look at the brahmin girl and was instantly smitten. She was quite a looker, and there was something about the way she held herself, a sense of dignity and pride that was almost regal. In richer clothes and bejewelled, she could have passed for a princess. In fact, she was more attractive than any of the Nanda princesses!

The little brahmin boy, her brother, saw Chandra staring at his sister and screwed up one eye with an expression that suggested he knew why Chandra was staring and didn't like it. He kept staring at Chandra till Chandra shrugged and smiled back.

Chandra didn't usually stare at the marks. That's what they were after all: marks for him and his fellow Cuts to aim for and steal from. Looking too closely humanised them. And attracted unwanted attention to oneself. Like the little boy who had noticed him ogling his big sister and was giving him a warning look now. But the girl and her family were so innocent, fresh, decent. The last several months in Pataliputra had exposed him to so many undesirables that he had almost forgotten there were still decent people left in the world. Like this family. They reminded him in a way of his own family, when he was about that boy's age. Back home. When it had still been home.

He wallowed for a moment in his nostalgia.

Suddenly, he saw something which snapped him out of his spell.

Somatose's goons. They had seen the eldest daughter too. Their leers made it clear they shared Chandra's appreciation for her looks. It made Chandra's stomach clench to see them ogling her, but it was only natural. But then they began to follow the family, and he knew what that meant.

Cutting was only one tiny part of Maha-amatya's sources of income. Chandra had no idea how much the Prime Minister earned from pickpocketing in the entire Lower City, though he knew it was substantial; yet this income paled in comparison to the profits from other enterprises. Especially one in particular: trafficking. The market in young boys and girls was a perennially flourishing one; some Cuts even started in that line of work, then sometimes worked their way up to Cutting when they were a little older. The Cut who had been found face down in the cesspool had been one such boy. The boy had been the pet of a certain Minister in the Emperor's court for the past several months. But once he began showing the inevitable signs of maturity, the Minister had discarded him like a soiled napkin. He had never been able to fully adjust to Cutting; while he learned the craft well enough, he had grown too accustomed to the comforts and luxuries that a pet enjoyed in his master's service, and resented losing those perks and adapting to the gritty, low-rent life of a Cut. Rumour was that he had offered to let out secrets about the Minister and that was what had gotten him killed. It had happened the night after he had gone on a drunken rant and muttered 'Rakshasa' so bitterly. Chandra had spent some time with him, picking up useful information about the various nether-worldly goings-on of the city. Among the things he had picked up was insight into the lucrative trafficking business. Which was why he knew that those two goons weren't just leching at the eldest daughter of the brahmin family but had more sinister designs on her.

Chandra followed the goons and the brahmin family for several minutes, long enough to be certain that he had read the situation correctly. When he saw the two men talking and making certain signs to one another he knew his suspicions were well founded.

They intended to abduct the girl.

He cursed softly, drawing disapproving looks from an elderly rishi leading a group of young acolytes. He didn't waste time apologising to the priest for his blasphemy. From what he knew of this dark business, it would be only a short while before that girl was taken from her family, never to be seen alive by them again.

Chandra had seen it done more than once since he had begun working for Rakshasa. Each time he had witnessed it, he had felt sickened to the core. He had once seen a similar abduction in another smaller city and had left that place that very same day, unable to stomach such sights. Cutting was not exactly the most honourable profession, but at worst, he was parting people from their money and valuables, nothing more than that. Trafficking parted them from their right to consent, and their lives. He had seen the girls in Red Lamp Area: what had been taken from them could never be earned again or put into a purse. And those were the luckier ones. He had heard stories about those taken to the High Houses, about the goings-on there. And the palace? No one returned alive from there. Especially if taken to certain of the Nanda princes. This brahmin girl was attractive enough to end up there. She was beautiful enough to be a prince's toy, to be used and then discarded when the royal tired of her. The very idea revolted Chandra.

He followed the family and the goons while trying to think quickly of some way to prevent this from happening.

It helped that he knew their methods, step by step.

'First, they distract the father, or husband, or whoever else she's travelling with,' the other Cut had told him one night. 'Then, while the father's distracted, they make her unconscious and vanish her.'

'How?' Chandra had asked, curious.

The Cut had been habituated to smoking hookah, a habit he had picked up from his former High House master; there were no hookahs in Lower City, so he made do with smoking vile-smelling little sticks made of dried tobacco leaves stuffed with spiced tobacco. He took a long puff and exhaled the smoke. 'Mostly, they use a cloth wetted with a liquid dose of a drug; puts you to sleep at once if inhaled. Wake up with a really bad headache.' He gazed at the swirling smoke. 'How they took me from my family.' He took another angry puff and went on. 'They pull you into an alley and stuff you in a sack. After that, you're merchandise to be transported wherever.'

Chandra watched the goons' hands carefully. Neither of them had a cloth in his hand yet or a vial of liquid, so they were not yet ready to drug and snatch her. He guessed they were waiting for the distraction. He racked his brains trying to think of which would be the best spot to do it then snapped his fingers, again startling the rishi who was muttering a mantra repeated by his acolytes to protect them from the temptations all around.

'Hanuman Peth!' Chandra said.

That was the place they would take her—unless he did something to stop it.

7

Vishnu saw the older boy again. The first time, he had been staring at Menaka, Vishnu's elder sister, with that look older boys often got when they saw her. Vishnu didn't like anyone looking at his sister like that, as if she was a tasty savoury and they were hungry dogs. The older boy had seen Vishnu glaring at him and had flashed him a smile. Vishnu hadn't been taken in by the smile. He had continued to glare, letting the older boy know in no uncertain terms that looking at his sisters—any of his sisters—with a hungry-dog look was not acceptable. The boy had disappeared after that and Vishnu had forgotten about him. There were so many things to see on his first trip to the big city.

He was enjoying simply walking along, holding Menaka's hand, and doing that thing he always did when there too many things to take in at once: he looked straight ahead, turning his head from time to time to see both sides of the street. This way he could take in the entire street, not looking at any one thing or person in particular, but absorbing all of it. He had been doing this all along their journey. Later, maybe that evening, or whenever he wished, he would simply think back to those moments and recall the sights. And it would be as if he were walking this street again, seeing everything, then be able to stop at leisure, look at something more closely, or at someone, and consider that item or person at length. Everything stayed in his mind, as clear as if he were looking at it again for the first time.

This was how he memorised his lessons. Once he heard a shloka, or a paksha, or even a full kaand recited aloud, it went straight into his brain. He could recall and recite it back verbatim, word for word, syllable for syllable, down to the last matra. He knew that other children—other people too—didn't possess this ability, and that people in the village thought it made him special. To Vishnu, it was simply the way he was and had always been. Was a pebble special because it was smooth and round? It was simply made that way! Vishnu had been made this way.

When he saw the boy again, he recognised him at once. Or rather his brain did. It was a reflexive thing. He saw the boy appear seemingly from nowhere, this time ahead of Vishnu and his family, which was strange, and knew at once that this one face was a familiar one amongst all the hundreds of faces on the same street.

The boy had appeared from a narrow gap between two stalls. Vishnu saw a dark space behind the stalls, which suggested an alley between the shops. The boy had burst out from there suddenly, but had then slowed and slunk down, as if hiding from someone. Vishnu focused on the boy's eyes and tracked his gaze: the boy wasn't looking at Menaka. He was looking at someone on the other side of the street, just behind Vishnu's family. Vishnu turned and looked that way and at once saw what the boy had been looking at.

Two full-grown men, older than Menaka but younger than Vishnu's father and mother, were following them. They were looking at Menaka too: staring at her with strange expressions. Their expressions were different from the usual hungry-dog looks Menaka got. These two men had the look of dogs who had seen the savoury and were very hungry, but knew they could not simply run and grab it. Like the village dog, Raja, that Vishnu had once seen stealing a savoury from Shantaram's shop. Shantaram had just fried the savouries and set the whole platter out to cool. Then Shantaram sat on small wooden stool beside the platter, to guard it as well as to call out that he had hot fresh savouries to sell.

Vishnu had been walking at that exact moment and had seen Raja skulking across the street. Vishnu had stopped, sensing a coup in the offing. Right enough, Raja had carefully eyed the heaped platter and smacked his chops, a little drool dribbling from the sides of his grinning jaws. Then Raja had done the clever thing that Vishnu had admired so much. Had Raja simply darted across the street to grab a savoury, Shantaram would have raised his stick and whacked poor Raja. Instead, Raja had gone behind the house, then around the next house, then crossed the street further up, out of Shantaram's immediate range of view. He had then gone behind the houses on Shantaram's side of the street and finally come out through the alley right behind Shantaram. Then, when Shantaram was distracted for a moment, standing up to gesture Vishnu and the other boys from the gurukul walking home, Raja the dog had darted around Shantaram's stool, nipped one of the savouries between his teeth, and darted back into the alley. So neatly was this done that when Shantaram sat back on his stool a moment later, he was none the wiser that one of his savouries had even been stolen! Vishnu had admired Raja's sly technique and become a fan of the dog after that day, making it his habit to bring him a little tidbit from time to time.

These men had the same look as Raja had when he saw Shantaram bringing out the platter of savouries.

What did that mean?

Menaka was not a savoury. They weren't dogs.

And why was the boy watching the men while they watched Menaka?

Vishnu's brain churned, sifting through the possibilities. Almost instantly, his mind came up with the only possible explanation: The men wanted to steal Menaka.

Why they would want to do that, he didn't know.

But there was no other explanation.

Because of his perfect memory, Vishnu remembered seeing the two men before as well. They had been around the same place where he had first seen the boy. And then later... He realised now that the men had been following his family. That would not seem unusual in itself since there were a lot of people walking in the same direction as Vishnu and his family, and he recognised all their faces as well. But the boy, the way he looked at them, that made it unusual.

It was the way Shantaram had looked at Raja. A look that said: No. You are not going to steal my savouries today. I won't let that happen.

Vishnu glanced at the boy again. He had moved closer now, and was looking at Vishnu's father with a different expression. It was an expression people had on their faces when they met someone for the first time: polite, friendly, nice.

The boy was going to speak to Vishnu's father in a moment, he could see that. But about what? Why? And what did that have to do with the two men and the odd way they were staring at Menaka?

Vishnu tugged at Menaka's hand. 'Didi, didi, listen.'

'What is it, Vish?' Menaka was looking at a display of colourful fabrics hanging on a stall nearby.

'Look at me, didi.'

Menaka sighed and turned her head to look down at him. 'What?'

He pointed with his chin over his shoulder. 'Those men are following us and staring at you.'

Menaka glanced briefly in the direction of the men. 'Which men? There are so many people here, I can't tell.'

'The ones who aren't brahmins. They look a little like Naveen and Varada from our village.'

She shrugged. 'I can't see anyone who looks like Naveen and Varada from our village.'

'I don't mean exactly like them. I mean the same sort of men.'

'What sort is that?' she asked impatiently, already losing interest and glancing back towards the hanging fabrics.

He tugged her hand again. 'Like they've been drinking that awful-smelling thing. Like they're going to get into a fight again. You know, like bad men.'

Menaka shook her head. 'Vishnu, as usual, I have absolutely no clue what you're talking about. Is this another one of your pranks? Are you going to tell me this is something you read in the Vedas or the epics again? Something one of the great gurus did, what are they called?'

'Saptarishis. No, didi, this is serious. Those men are going to do something bad.'

She frowned. 'Going to do? How can you know what they're going to do if they haven't done it yet?'

'Because…' he began trying to explain to her. But before he could finish, a loud noise from up the street startled them.

✍

Chandra stepped out in front of the father of the brahmin family. 'Namaskar, punditji.'

The pundit looked at him curiously. 'Namaskar.' He continued to walk up the street.

Chandra stepped in front of the pundit. 'Punditji, my name is Chandra. I wish to warn you. There are bad men looking to abduct your daughter.'

The pundit stopped at once, looking wary. 'Who are you?'

'Just a well-wisher. The men I speak of have arranged for a distraction a little way ahead. While your wife and you are distracted, they mean to snatch your eldest girl and make off with her.'

'What?' The pundit looked back at his family. His wife had not heard Chandra's words because of all the noise in the street, but she saw her husband looking back and frowned. The pundit was a little reassured when he saw his eldest daughter, still clutching her little brother's hand, then turned back to Chandra.

'Why are you telling me this?' he asked.

'I wish to help you, punditji,' Chandra said. 'They are very bad men. You must not let them take your girl.'

The pundit glanced around nervously. Clearly, he was a scholarly man, unaccustomed to worldly problems and ignorant of the darker underworld of the big city. 'What should I do?' he asked.

'Do exactly as I say...' Chandra began. But before he could finish, a loud noise sounded up the street.

It was the sound of a metal thali being dropped on the stone steps that led up to the Hanuman temple for which Hanuman Peth was named. The street bifurcated about 20 yards ahead, both lanes curving around a small hillock. Stone steps had been cut into the front of the hillock, leading up to a Hanuman Temple. Along either side of the stone stairway were small stalls selling objects required for worship at the temple:

flowers, sarees, amulets and other trinkets, and metal thalis in which to carry the offerings. A boy had dropped several thalis on the stone steps, causing the loud noise. The thalis struck the steps, resounding and clanging deafeningly. The stall owner immediately added his voice to the cacophony, shouting loudly at the boy. The boy shouted back, complaining it wasn't his fault. The thalis meanwhile clattered and slid down to strike several pilgrims on their way up to worship at the temple; they also began calling out and lamenting. The milling crowds slowed and paused to stare up at the disarray, smiling at the spectacle.

Chandra knew this was the pre-planned disturbance. The boy was a Cut, one of his colleagues from this sector, and he worked the Hanuman Peth itself, a very lucrative location because of all the donations and offerings brought by the worshippers. He had probably been signalled by the goons to start the disturbance. Which meant that they were moving to take the girl!

Chandra clutched the pundit's arm. 'Quickly! Take hold of your daughter!'

The pundit turned, and Chandra was able to see the rest of the family. The wife was still clutching the hands of her younger daughters, and the eldest daughter was holding the hand of her little brother and staring ahead at the commotion on the temple steps. But behind them, Chandra saw the two goons only a few feet away from their target. He saw the objects in their hands, and the way they were moving and his heart sank.

I'm too late, Chandra thought.

8

The instant Vishnu heard the clattering of the thalis and the commotion on the steps, he saw the two bad men moving toward Menaka. One of them had a small container of some kind in one hand and as he approached, he emptied the liquid from the container onto a cloth he was holding in his other hand. He brought the cloth up as he came up from behind Menaka. The other man was shaking out a black gunnysack, holding it upside down with the mouth open as if he meant to place it over something.

Vishnu had no idea why the men had those items in their hands or what they intended to do, but he knew it had something to do with Menaka and whatever it was, it was not good.

He had a split second to react. He could have shouted to Menaka to watch out, or to move aside, or to run. But she was his elder sister and not given to instantly obeying orders shouted by him. The men were moving in so quickly, he knew that they would do what they intended to do within moments, like the dog Raja snatching up the savoury under Shantaram's very nose. He was not strong or big enough to stop the men if they tried to hurt Menaka or snatch her, and had only moments to do something.

So he did the only thing he could do.

Vishnu turned back toward the men, and pointed behind them.

He shouted at the top of his voice: 'Mad bull! Run!'

He shrieked the words, putting as much fear and alarm into his voice as he could muster. Which, since he was a seven-year-old boy, was quite a lot.

∽

Chandra saw the two goons reaching for the girl just as her little brother suddenly spun around and began shrieking.

'MAD BULL! RUN!'

Instantly, the crowd reacted. It was common for bulls and cows to lose their heads and start stampeding in a crowded street. Everyone knew the danger and the havoc an animal could cause with those deadly horns and pounding hooves. At once, the argument on the temple steps was forgotten, a minor distraction, and everyone began looking around to spot the errant bull. Where was it? Which direction was it headed? Where should they run to get out of its way?

The first persons to react were the two goons. They were only a foot away from the little boy when he began shrieking. They reacted as if stung by bees, stopping dead in their tracks, then turning around reflexively, because the boy was pointing behind them. So sincere was the little boy's shrieking that for a moment even Chandra was taken in. He began to scan the street to spot the bull.

Then his better sense kicked in. How could a little boy who was walking toward the Hanuman Peth possibly see a bull coming from behind? Chandra felt his own jaw drop in amazement. The boy was creating his own distraction! How utterly brilliant!

Confirming Chandra's suspicion, the instant the two goons turned around to look for the bull, the little brahmin pulled his sister's hand urgently, saying something to her that Chandra couldn't catch. The girl's eyes widened. She looked at once for her father. To his credit, the Pundit was also intelligent and gestured frantically to his eldest daughter, urging her to come to him.

The girl responded at once, running forward to join her father and Chandra. The mother and two little girls also came forward at once, sensing something amiss.

'Quickly,' Chandra said to them. 'Get in here!'

He was standing next to a line of stalls. They all had tables covered with thick cloth, on which they had set out their displays. The cloth hung down in front of the tables, which were all joined edge to edge, and Chandra picked up the end of a cloth and raised it, pointing to the space under the table.

The little boy was the smartest. 'Do as he says! Hide!'

He pulled his sister's hand, yanking her down. With a glance at Chandra, she ducked under the table top and crouched underneath. The pundit, his wife and two daughters followed. Chandra dropped the cloth, which made the entire family disappear from sight, and shoved his hands into the pockets of his vastra, acting like he was scanning the crowd for marks.

Out the corner of his eye, he saw the two goons turning around, surprised to see that the girl they had been only a foot away from a moment ago, had vanished. The crowd had continued moving through the street, taking up the space occupied a moment ago by the brahmin family. 'There's no bull!' someone called out. The crowd laughed uncertainly, then continued moving. The commotion at the temple steps had subsided as well, with the Cut having run off as he had been told to do.

The two goons looked around the street in every direction, confused. They grabbed a few shoulders, ran this way and that way, then finally accepted that somehow the family had vanished from sight.

They were moving in Chandra's direction, still scanning the crowd ahead in case their mark had walked away while their back was turned. One of them saw Chandra and he came forward.

'See a pundit and his family? Young girl with them, ripe one?'

Chandra frowned. 'The one with three or four daughters and a little boy?'

'That's them all right,' said the other goon. 'Where did they go? They were just here a moment ago.'

Chandra turned his head, looking in the direction of Hanuman Peth. The crowd was dividing at the temple steps, half going left, the other half going right. A few went up the steps to the temple itself, probably to ask the son of the wind god for his blessings before they undertook whatever business had brought them to Pataliputra. Chandra said a quick prayer himself, silently.

He turned back, frowning as if still unsure. 'They went up that way. Not sure if they went left or right...or up to the temple.'

The two goons pushed past him without a word, one elbowing him in the chest.

Chandra rubbed the spot, saying softly, 'You're welcome, donkeyface.'

He saw them pause at the foot of the temple steps, arguing briefly about which way to go. Finally, they remembered the advantage of having two persons and split up, each going one way. The instant they vanished from sight, Chandra squatted down and raised the edge of the table cloth.

'They're gone, you can come out now.'

They emerged warily. Chandra offered his hand to each one and they took it, all except the little boy who looked at him sharply. The intelligence in the boy's eyes reminded Chandra of someone but he couldn't place who at this moment. His mind was more concerned with how to get them away from this place before the goons decided to come back this way.

'We have to get you away from this sector,' he told the father.

The Pundit looked around uncertainly. 'I don't understand all this. Who were those men, and who are you? Why are you helping us?'

He looked at Chandra with an expression that conveyed what he had left unsaid: What's in it for you?

Chandra nodded. 'You are right to be suspicious of me. I am only seeking to help you. As for why,' he paused. 'I lost my sister,' he admitted. 'Back home in my hometown, not here. She was taken just the way they tried to take your daughter. My father and mother went to try and get her back and...' he shook his head. 'They were killed.'

The mother put her hand over her mouth, horrified. 'Who are these men?'

'They are bad men who do this for a living.' Chandra glanced around at the crowded street. 'We have to get you away from this sector in case they come back. They have people everywhere who work for them. Any one of them could see you and tell them. Come with me.'

He led them through a gap between the stalls that led to an alleyway. It was a narrow walkway that ran alongside one of the canals that conveyed the city's sewage down to the river; the smell was awful but it was the only way to get off the street from here.

'Ignore the smell,' he told them, then pointed to the end of the walkway. 'Go to the end, then turn left, and you will get out in the next sector.'

'But I am here to attend the conference.' the Pundit said.

'And you can attend it. I'll find a way to throw those men off your track. They only work in this sector, so once you're out of here, you will be fine. Just make sure you don't come back this way, and while you're in the city, don't leave your daughter unattended. Better yet, have her wear a veil. It's for her own protection, believe me.'

The Punditji clasped his hand. 'Thank you, son. You are a good soul. You will be blessed for helping us today.'

They went by Chandra, the eldest daughter looking at him keenly as she passed by. The last one to go by was the little boy and he stopped and stared up at Chandra with a fierce glare.

'What is your name, boy?' he asked in the squeaky voice of little boys.

Chandra arched his eyebrows at the boy's tone and at the way he called someone a good decade older 'boy'. 'Chandra, little man. What's your name?'

'Vishnu Gupta,' he said, then followed his family.

Chandra watched till they were safely around the corner then slipped back onto the street.

He grinned to himself, shaking his head. That little boy was quite a character. If he hadn't shouted "Mad Bull!" at that moment, he would have lost his sister forever. He was one to watch out for!

He slipped into the crowd, returning to work. He still had a quota to fill and the day was more than half gone. He had to find something worth filching—and soon—or else the sector leader would have his hide.

He moved through the streets, looking for marks even as he Cut the occasional pocket here and there.

A few hours later, he reported back to the sector leader. The man was in a bad mood. His goons were standing in front of him and he had evidently been giving them a good dressing down. Their faces were surly. They saw Chandra and pointed him out. At once, Chandra's heart skipped.

'Ask Chandra, he knows, he was right there,' said one of them.

Somatose turned to glare at Chandra. 'Well?'

Holy mother of Vishnu, I'm caught good and proper now.

'What have you got to say for yourself then?' Somatose asked, prodding him with his finger.

Chandra took out the cloth purse and tossed it on the table. It landed with a satisfying metallic thump. 'There you go. How's that for something of value?'

The sector leader frowned and prodded the purse. 'What is that? Never seen a purse like this before.'

'It's silk. That's what the Chinn priests use, because they don't like purses made of cow hide leather. Go on, open it and take a look.'

The leader did as he suggested, emptying the contents of the silk purse on the table top. The coins gleamed and shone in the evening light. He picked one up, staring at the curious symbols on it. 'What coin is this?'

'Chinn coin,' Chandra said, resisting the urge to add 'obviously'. 'He must have been the high priests of their order or something.'

'Is this real gold?' the man asked, then tested a coin by biting it between his half-rotted teeth. Chandra thought the man was lucky it was real gold; if it had been more than half iron, he would probably have lost one of his last four or five teeth. 'Well, I'll be.' He poured the coins back into the purse. 'Not bad. Not bad at all for an otherwise lacklustre day.'

He saw the two goons staring at the purse and scowled at them. 'No thanks to you two! Lost me a week's worth of Cutting, you two did!'

The goons pointed again at Chandra. 'Ask him. He saw how that family skedaddled. They must have run like mad up Hanuman Peth. We looked everywhere but they were gone. Vanished.'

'One moment they were there, within hand's reach,' said the other man, 'the next minute they were gone with the wind.'

'You're talking about the brahmin family?' Chandra asked with fake innocence. 'The one you asked me about near Hanuman Peth?'

'That's the one!' said the goon.

'They must have panicked when someone shouted "Mad Bull". They ran like mad people.'

The sector leader frowned. 'What mad bull?'

'The boy,' said the goon. 'The little brahmin. He yelled it just as we were about to grab the girl. We turned back to look for a moment, and when we turned back, they were all gone.'

'Yes,' Chandra said, 'that's what happened.'

The sector leader slapped one of his goons with an open palm. 'Fool!'

'Hey, boss! What was that for?'

'You son of a goat! They were on to you. That's why the boy shouted "Mad Bull!" There wasn't any bull, was there?'

The goons looked at each other.

'His father must have seen you and figured your intentions,' Somatose went on. 'What did you say he was? A merchant?'

'A pundit,' Chandra said helpfully.

'Right, a pundit. Some of these pundits are smart. They must have seen you two lurking and leering at the girl. So the father tells son to yell out and you two were fooled by the yell. Then they skedaddled up Hanuman Peth.'

The goons were frowning.

'But then where did they go? There were only two ways to go from there and we covered them both.'

'And we were real careful like,' said the other one, the one who had been in charge of applying the drugged cloth to the girl's face to make her unconscious. 'We were behind them and never saw them look back once. The father never even saw us properly.'

'We do good work,' said the first, the one who had carried the gunnysack. 'We've done this a dozen, two dozen times before. Never been anything like today.'

'Yeah, Chandra was there, he'll tell you,' said the second man.

Chandra nodded. 'I didn't even realise these guys were there until they came up and asked me about the girl.'

The sector leader shook his head, waving them all away dismissively. 'Forget it. I'm tired of all your excuses. At least my boy Chandra here brought me something worth passing up the line. There's going to be a happy face up top tonight.' He jerked his head in the direction of the mansion at the top of the hillside on which Lower City was spread. 'And I'll have a little extra commission to buy an extra jug of honey wine. The good stuff.'

He wagged a filthy finger in the faces of the two goons. 'I would have shared too. But you fools let me down. Cost me a pretty penny in profits. A girl like that, if she was half of what you say she was, would fetch a week's worth of Cuts. But you let her slip out your fingers. So you can get back out there and keep looking for another one. It's conference season and we need more fresh girls. You know the quota. Go on. Get back to work.'

The two goons looked unhappy, but knew better than to argue further. They shrugged and glared at the leaders back as he shuffled off to buy himself some of the 'better stuff' he had been talking about.

The goons came past Chandra, muttering to themselves. The taller one who usually held the gunnysack paused and turned back. 'You're sure you saw them running up Hanuman Peth?' he asked. 'Because we searched all the way to the end of the Peth and never saw hide nor hair of them.'

Chandra shrugged. 'I saw them running, don't know which way they went. Like I told you.'

The man stared at Chandra a moment longer, then turned abruptly and followed after his associate.

Chandra heaved a sigh of relief, daubing the sweat that had oozed from under his arms and from his forehead. That had been close.

He went to the little hut behind the wine shop where he and the other Cut boys slept each night. It was a hovel; just an empty hut with straw pallets laid on the ground. He knew the other boys would have gone to get something to eat, or to drink. Most Cuts drank heavily, even the younger boys, and Chandra had his days too when all he wanted was to drown himself in liquor and forget all the things he saw and heard and knew that caused him pain. But not tonight. Tonight, he had bigger things to worry about than just eating and drinking.

He had been seen talking to the brahmin family on the street near Hanuman Peth. All the stall owners and traders in the sector knew him, not by name, but as one of the Cut boys. They knew he worked for the sector boss, same as the two goons.

They knew the two goons lifted pretty girls and boys. They knew everything that went on in the sector, often under their noses, and kept quiet about it, because if they didn't, they would end up in a cesspool facedown. They hadn't said anything today, figuring that he was on some odd errand. Theirs was not to question or wonder why. But if those two goons went back to Hanuman Peth and began asking questions, sooner or later, someone would mention that this one Cut boy had been acting oddly.

Oddly how, the goons would ask.

Well, he hid the family under the table cloth, then he took them out again and told them to go through the shortcut, you know, the walkway by the sewage canal, the one which leads to the next sector.

And that would be enough. The goons would figure out the rest.

They weren't smart like pundits. No Vedas and Vedangas had ever passed their cracked lips and rotting teeth. But they were street smart. They knew when a fast one was being pulled on them, and they would know at once that Chandra had been the one responsible for letting the girl slip out of their clutches today.

And when they realised that, they would bring the information straight to the sector boss.

Who would then tell them to beat Chandra to a pulp, and then have him sent up on top. To the big boss up there. Rakshasa. And what Rakshasa would do was not in any doubt at all. Chandra knew what happened to anyone who crossed Rakshasa even slightly. Down to the dungeon. What was it the Maha-amatya liked to say? Suffering and death. That was what would happen to Chandra once he found out. A great deal of suffering and a slow, very painful death.

Some of the other Cuts came in, asking him if he had eaten yet. They were off to have a round or two and invited him to join them. He ignored them; they abused him, then left.

Even now, as he lay here on his pallet, scratching at the lice bites, those two goons could be at the very stall where he had hidden the family under a table. Asking the questions that would lead to Chandra's end.

He sat up.

He had to do something quick.

Before they found out.

And it had to make the entire problem go away.

The only way to do that was to make the goons go away. Both of them.

Once they were dead, nobody else would bother to question the stall owners on Hanuman Peth. Why would they? Only the two goons had been there and had seen Chandra near the family. The stall owners and other merchants would keep their mouths shut, unless asked a direct question. And no one but the two goons would know the right questions to ask.

Yes, the more he thought about it, the more he realised that the only way he could be sure of not getting caught was by getting rid of the two goons.

He would have to kill them both. Tonight. Before they found out what he had done, and reported it to the sector boss.

Chandra rose from his pallet. His day was not yet over. He had work to do, the dirtiest, bloodiest kind of work there was on earth. Murder.

9

By the third day of the conference, Vishnu was unspeakably bored. The first day he had been so excited. His father and he had left Vishnu's mother and sisters in the camp where tents had been provided for the attendees to live in. There were thousands of brahmins everywhere, and as they had walked across the large open field to the much larger tents where the sammelan was taking place, he had felt a thrill of anticipation. He was even able to put aside his irritation at learning that his mother and sisters were not permitted to attend.

'Why can't they come too?' he had asked his father when he learned that only the two of them would actually go to attend the conference.

'Because only men are allowed,' his father had explained patiently.

'Yes, but why?'

His father had sighed. 'That's just the way things are, Vishnu.'

'Well, that's not the way they should be.'

'Be that as it may, it is the way they are, and as visitors, we have to respect that rule. Now let us go or we will be late.'

'Don't worry about us, my son,' his mother said, kissing him on the top of his head. 'I am looking forward to exchanging news and information with all the other wives here from so many different places.'

'And we don't want to sit and listen to those boring, old white-beards talking all day about Vedas and Puranas,' Menaka had said.

'We don't want to listen to white beards!' her younger sisters chorused.

'Come now, Vishnu, we must not be late on the first day,' his father prompted.

He had left, reluctantly.

But as he walked across the field, alongside what looked like a sea of other white and red ochre-clad brahmins of all ages, he had felt the unjustness of the 'men-only rule' leave him. A thrill of anticipation rushed through his body.

The sun was shining, birds were flying overhead, and the bustle and attractions of the great city of Pataliputra lay all around him, but to Vishnu, those large tents up ahead were the real attraction. The idea of spending day after day with the world's greatest scholars and thinkers, talking about scriptures and knowledge, was more thrilling than any mela or fair. To him, knowledge and debate were more exciting than anything else in life. This was the most thrilling thing he had ever done in his short life. It was swarga, pure swarga!

His father and he reached the sammelan tents and began looking into first one, then the next. Vishnu peeked in with him. Each tent was already filled to capacity with dozens of brahmins, most already seated cross-legged on straw mats on the ground, facing a central red ochre cloth where the main speakers were seated, waiting for the talk to begin; new arrivals moved through the lines of seated brahmins, searching for places to sit.

After they had peeked into a half dozen tents, Vishnu grew impatient. 'Why don't we just sit in any one?'

His father glanced at him with a small smile. 'Because these are all for brahmins.'

'I'm a brahmin!' Vishnu replied.

His father looked around the field, searching for something. 'You're a brahmacharya. You will be a brahmin in time, but you're still an acolyte, Vishnu.'

'That isn't fair. I already know more than most brahmins in our village!'

'Well, this isn't our village, is it? This is Pataliputra. They have different rules and standards here, and we have to respect them.'

His father finally saw something and went toward a particular group of tents. Vishnu saw other white-clad brahmacharyas like himself entering these tents. There were almost no red ochre-clad grown-up brahmins. A suspicion dawned on him. When he reached the tent and looked in, he scowled.

'This is it,' his father said, 'go on in, I'll come at the end of the day and we'll walk home together.'

'You want me to sit with the children?' Vishnu asked.

His father sighed. 'Vishnu, look at yourself. You're seven years old. You are a child! In fact, you're probably one of the youngest here. Most gurukuls only allow pupils nine years or older to attend these events.'

'I'm smarter than all of them,' Vishnu said matter-of-factly, without any suggestion of superiority. 'Smarter than their gurus too.'

'Perhaps, but the rule isn't based on what's inside your head,' his father touched Vishnu's little bald head gently, 'it's based on your age. If anyone asks your age, just tell them your guru brought you here. And in the name of the Holy Trimurti, please don't get into any arguments with the speakers. These are all highly respected gurus and I don't want to hear complaints about misbehaviour.'

'I never misbehave!' Vishnu said, outraged.

'That depends on each person's definition of misbehaviour. Showing off to your teacher is a form of misbehaviour too.' His father looked around. Most of the brahmins and brahmacharyas had gone inside the tents, leaving the field almost empty. 'I have to go now or my talk will begin. I'm a featured speaker. Be good, Vishnu!'

Vishnu watched his father hurry away to the grown-up tents. Punditji found his tent and ducked under the flap. Vishnu remained standing with his hands on his hips, fists clenched. He couldn't believe that he had to sit with the children. How humiliating!

Two young boys, one almost twice his height, the other almost twice his width, came up in a hurry and pushed past him, going in. Vishnu glared at them but they were oblivious, like most young boys their age. Did people not grow brains until grey began appearing in their hair? It often seemed like it to him. Then again, even some greybeards didn't seem to be very brainy in his experience. At least his family was intelligent, but outside the house he rarely had anyone to talk to. Except, of course, Vaishali. The thought of his friend made him smile and it was with that smile on his face that he finally entered the tent, too short to need to even duck under the flap.

The tent was packed with boys older and bigger than Vishnu, all seated cross-legged in neat rows. It was like gurukul, but five times the gurukul in his village. No, he corrected himself, scanning the tent quickly, not five times, only four and two-tenths as large. Four and three-tenths if you counted the half dozen much older boys sitting behind the gurus. What were they sitting there for?

'If we have finished examining the premises, may we all take our seats, please?'

Vishnu looked up.

The guru was addressing the class, but looking at him.

So was every other pair of eyes in the tent.

Vishnu had seen other brahmacharyas back in the village gurukul when they arrived late to class. They slunk in nervously like little mice, trying to sneak past the teacher's gaze and sit before he noticed them. But he always noticed them. Obviously. Vishnu didn't understand the need to skulk and sneak in when you were obviously visible. He always simply walked in and sat down. It was more dignified and honest.

He looked around calmly, searching for a suitable place to sit.

All the rows were full except for one: This one seemed to be exactly the same length as the others, but there was in fact one boy less in the row. The large boy who had just pushed past him with his taller friend was sitting in this row and for some reason the boys on either side had left him several inches of space.

Vishnu walked to the end of that row and said politely, 'Move up.'

The boys sitting at the end nearest to him began a sideways wriggling motion as he shifted to make space. Other boys passed on the movement, until the boy nearest to the large one reluctantly sidled a little closer to his much larger neighbor. The large boy, however, did not budge an inch. This left about half as much space for Vishnu at the end of the row as all the other boys occupied. Vishnu was almost half the size of most of the other boys so he could have made do with this little space, but he had no intention of simply making do.

He snapped his fingers, aiming the action at the very large boy in the middle of the row. 'You, sir. Please move up.'

The large boy's very large head swivelled slowly. Two very small eyes, disproportionate to the face in which they were placed, stared down at Vishnu. Even seated, the large boy was taller than Vishnu standing up. He stared without any expression at Vishnu for a moment, then lifted one rear cheek, using both his hands, put it down two or three inches to the right, then repeated the process with his other rear cheek. Vishnu gestured to the other boys in the row who reluctantly moved another two or three inches further up. Vishnu now felt satisfied. He bent down to dust off the straw mat, then finally took his seat, arranging himself comfortably.

When he looked up, the guru and all the six older brahmacharyas seated behind him were glaring at him.

Vishnu's face widened at once in a pleasant smile.

The guru shook his head and looked away. The six teacher's assistants kept glaring.

Vishnu dropped the smile and sighed inwardly. It was going to be a long day.

And it had been.

As had the next two days after that.

Everything being said, or discussed, or debated, was of such a basic level that Vishnu could have handled it three or four years ago. A child of four could understand this level of instruction! Well, perhaps not any child of four, but certainly Vishnu Gupta at age four. To him, it was as basic as the alphabet now. He had moved far, far beyond this level.

Back home in gurukul, he had simply interrupted the teacher and asked questions at a time like this. Under the pretext of wanting to know more, he would posit certain queries in such a way so that the teacher, in order to answer Vishnu, would have to discuss things that were of a much higher level than the actual lesson. Before the teacher could fully answer that first question, Vishnu would pose another, and then another, elevating the discussion a step up each time. In this way, he prompted discussions with the teacher at a far higher level than the class—and often, at a level higher than even the teacher's own knowledge! It was his way of tricking the teacher into bypassing the actual lesson and engaging in what amounted to a one-on-one tuition session with his most intelligent student. The teacher never saw through this trick because Vishnu was clever enough to always speak in a wide-eyed innocent manner that made it seem as though he had heard something somewhere which he didn't fully comprehend, and of course, the teacher's job was to educate him. It was only in the past year or so that the teacher had finally cottoned on to the ruse, and realised that Vishnu Gupta was effectively hijacking the class since none of the other students understood even a fragment of what they were discussing!

He tried the same ruse on the first day at the Pataliputra conference.

'No questions,' said one of the big boys sitting behind the guru. 'Guruji is speaking.'

Vishnu had frowned. 'But you ask questions.'

It was true. The six big boys who sat behind the guru were permitted to ask questions from time to time, which the guru would dutifully answer.

'We are seniors. Guruji has given his permission,' replied the big boys at once.

Vishnu understood. It was a scam. The big boys were all pupils of the guru, no doubt his oldest students from his gurukul. They had been prepped to ask questions at certain times, questions to which the guru had neat, previously prepared answers. This was all well and good in itself, but what irked Vishnu was that the guru didn't permit anyone else to ask any questions. What was the point of coming all the way to Pataliputra if you couldn't engage in open discussion?

He complained to his father at the end of the first tiresome day.

'I want to sit with you.'

His father sighed. 'You know you cannot. And you know why.'

'Tell them I'm your teacher's aide. All gurus have teacher's aides.'

'Yes, well, I'm a scholar, not a teacher as such. And you're too young to be a teacher's aide.'

'I can teach my class back home as well as Masterji can. I can explain the Vedangas better than this guru can! He and all his six aides!'

Punditji said firmly, 'What isn't possible isn't possible, Vishnu.'

So here he was now, on the third day of the conference, listening once again to the greybeard guru droning on. He was ready to yawn. He was ready to yawn, stretch out and fall asleep. It was so boring, he could have explained all these same things when he was four years old. Three, even. And now he had to sit here all day and listen to it again, without even being able to ask a question or start a discussion that tangentially progressed into more challenging areas.

And there were still weeks to go! They were to be here for a whole masa. Four whole weeks of this would drive him mad. He didn't know what the effect of prolonged repetition of the same mundane knowledge was on young minds, but he suspected it was related to the fact that all the other boys in this tent were listening with such rapt attention. Clearly, they had never had their minds challenged, had never questioned or even been taught to question, and that lack of challenge and failure to question had diminished their capacity to learn. They would plod along through the years, learning the pre-set lessons at the pre-set ages, finally going on to become competent purohits and agnihotris or whatever other sub-field of priest they were herded into by their parents and mentors. Like brahmin sheep, corralled and fenced.

When they broke for the morning meal, a vapid repast that comprised bland, nourishing food better suited to infants, Vishnu decided he had had enough. He would not be able to take another hour of this mindless monotony, never mind a whole four weeks.

When it was time for the lecture to resume, he delayed returning to the tent until all the other boys had gone in. He waited till he heard the monotonous drone of the guru's voice through the tent flaps. Then he walked away from the brahmacharya tents, across the field to the brahmin tents.

10

He had already checked the other brahmacharya tents during the previous two days, hoping to find at least one guru more open and engaging; he quickly learned that they were all the same. It was as if they had all been cast from the same mould; only their beards were slightly longer or shorter, whiter or greyer. Other than superficial differences, they might as well have been avatars of the same unexceptional being.

The field was empty now, everyone already inside the tents. The brahmin tents were larger and had several entrances. He made his way to the nearest one and peeked in. His height was an advantage: he was too small and close to the ground to be noticed even if he poked his entire head inside.

He saw a tent about thrice the size of the brahmacharya ones, but with about twice as many occupants. That was because adult brahmins tended to be somewhat larger than their younger brahmacharya counterparts; one of many disadvantages of growing up, in Vishnu's opinion.

Here too, the brahmins were all seated in neat concentric rows; they faced a central rectangular square in which sat several white-bearded gurus. There were no aides here. Rather than a single guru lecturing on a topic, they appeared to be discussing a scripture, each taking turns to comment on the passage.

Vishnu listened for a while, then moved on. The discussion itself was interesting, but the scripture wasn't one that held much interest for him. He paused at the entrances to several other tents, briefly auditing various discussions, until he found one that instantly captivated his attention.

He slipped into this tent, sitting behind the very last row. Because of the size of the grown-up brahmins in front of him, he didn't have a clear view of the gurus who were speaking. That was something he was used to. As the smallest boy in the brahmacharya tent, and as one of the smallest boys back in the village gurukul, he was used to not seeing the guru. Back in the village gurukul he had resolved this problem simply by sitting in the front row, often all by himself, since none of the other children wanted to sit next to him because he was constantly drawing the teacher's attention and they would be called out for fidgeting, or digging their noses, or some other distraction. Here, he had to manage mostly listening without seeing. Occasionally he was able to glimpse one of the gurus between the hulking backs of the brahmins in front of him, mainly when the men leaned this way or that way for a moment. This was sufficient. It was the discussion that he cared about, and he could hear it just fine.

One of the gurus was quoting from scriptures. Even before he finished the first shloka, Vishnu knew the source: Ayodhyakaand, Ramayana. The guru quoted a long extract, then launched into an interpretation of the verses. Another guru seated beside him discussed the interpretation and offered a few further observations. A third guru questioned some of these observations and suggested that some might find them questionable; but he went on to bolster them with his own analysis. The fourth guru—there were five of them in all— offered a variant view that was almost exactly the same as the first guru's interpretation. The fifth guru then asked a few questions before suggesting that the interpretation was very much in keeping with the canonical view and there was little to be added through further discussion. Even after saying this, the five of them still went on discussing the same passage, basically reiterating the same points over and over again with only subtle differences.

Vishnu began to grow weary of the repetition. He waited for someone to offer a challenge or even a contradiction. He could think of several. But the entire audience sat silently, simply listening to the five gurus. It was not very different from the guru lecturing the brahmacharyas in the boys' tents. Except that it apparently took five gurus repeating the same points to qualify for a grown-up conference. He waited eagerly for someone, anyone, to ask a question that challenged the gurus and brought some life back into this discussion. As the afternoon wore on, and the same rote recitations continued, he began to doubt any such questions would come.

Unexpectedly, a voice spoke up.

'All this is well and good, gurudev, but what about the real question?'

The discussion ceased abruptly. Everyone looked around to see who had asked the question.

The five gurus looked around the tent, their bearded hawk-like profiles turning in unison like a quintet of dance performers.

Finally one of them said patiently, 'What is the real question?'

'Did any of these events actually take place?'

A wave of murmurs swept across the tent. The beards of the gurus bristled. 'What an insolent question. Of course these events took place. Maharishi Valmiki has said they took place.'

'No, he does not. He says that he asked Lord Brahma how could he see everything that was taking place in so many places to so many people. Lord Brahma then said…,' and here the questioner interjected a long quote from an earlier passage, 'exhorting Maharishi Valmiki to go ahead and write all that came to his mind, and that all events would be made known to him, even those events which had yet to occur, and he would know all things that occurred to all people in the process of composition itself.'

There was a moment of silence; the entire tent was now listening with keen interest.

'Your interpretation is truncated but acceptable,' said one of the gurus, sniffing as if to show his disapproval of the brief summary, 'but what exactly is your question?'

'If the events had not yet taken place, and if Valmiki, by his own admission, was not present at all the locations where the events occurred, then how could he have possibly known of these events or of the experiences of the people involved in all the events? It is illogical.'

Another wave of murmurs, this one expressing consternation.

'That is a rude and highly contentious interpretation,' said one of the other gurus, his face flushed and eyes flashing. 'We cannot speak in such a manner of the great Maharishi Valmiki.'

'It is not an interpretation. It is a logical analysis of Maharishi Valmiki's own words. He tells us quite clearly that he was unsure of his own qualifications to tell such a momentous tale as that of Rama Chandra. Even Saptarishi Narada has to urge him repeatedly to undertake the work of composing the tale. And later, when he suffers a moment of acute self-doubt, Lord Brahma himself appears to him and has to exhort him to start composing, reassuring him that all that was needed to be known would be made known to him.' Another quote from

Valmiki, with some annotations on the shlokas and usage of Sanskrit by Brahma versus the construction of Valmiki's own shlokas. 'It appears to be quite logical to draw the conclusion that Valmiki did not have any actual experience of the events or people and simply wrote his version of the tale based on his own interpretations of what he thought had occurred, or, in the case of many events, especially the Uttarakand, had yet to occur in future.'

'And your point being?' one of the gurus asked in a frosty tone. This was the same guru who had sniffed earlier.

'That Valmiki himself admits that he did not actually see or hear the events in question, or even meet many of the persons of whom he wrote.'

'Again,' said the guru with the flashing eyes, 'I fail to see your point.'

'My point is that we have no empirical evidence that the events actually took place as Maharishi Valmiki described them, or that the persons he described actually matched his descriptions.'

'Patently self-contradictory,' said Sniffing Guru, 'Maharishi Valmiki's observations are themselves empirical evidence.'

'Not without corroboration from other observers. And why did he not simply speak to the persons themselves and include their own words and experiences in the tale?'

'The subjects?' said Sniffing Guru, 'Outrageous! Do you mean to suggest that Maharishi Valmiki should have stooped to the level of asking vanars and rakshasas and mere mortals to corroborate their experiences?'

'Why not? They were the ones living through the events. Not merely sitting in a distant ashram in the forest, composing a poem about them.'

An uproar erupted at this comment. Everyone began speaking at once.

The five gurus rose to their feet, shouting above the uproar.

'Who is this insolent brahmin? Rise to your feet. Show yourself!' shouted Flashing Eyes.

Slowly, the brahmin rose to his feet. 'Pranaam, gurudevs. I meant no offense. I merely studied the text and interpreted it as we are all trained to do. Indeed, as even Maharishi Krishna Dweipayana himself analysed it and recast it in his own words within the context of his own great composition named Jaya.'

Pin-drop silence.

Every pair of eyes in the tent was fixed on the speaker.

The five gurus stared at him for several moments in shocked silence.

Vishnu kept his palms joined and face suitably contrite. At the moment, his small face and cherubic cheeks made him appear positively angelic.

'You?' asked Sniffing Guru, 'You were quoting and interpreting Maharishi Valmiki? How is that possible?'

'Impossible!' scoffed Flashing Eyes, 'this little acolyte could not be the one who spoke. Who is the speaker? Stand up and present yourself like a good brahmin.'

'It is I, gurudev,' Vishnu said contritely. 'Again, I meant no offense. Maharishi Valmiki himself provides us with the tools we require to question his own work. He himself questions his own capacity to compose such a work. As he says...,' Vishnu rattled off another long quote from the prologue that preceded Ayodhyakaand. 'He himself questions Narada-muni about his suitability to write such a tale. It takes first Narada and then Brahma to convince him that he must do so. And only then does he undertake the task. Which is in itself a justification of the art of critical re-evaluation. Maharishi Valmiki is in essence telling us that all poets must question their own work, question their ability to write, question their methodology, their means of gathering knowledge, and of ensuring the veracity of that knowledge. The fact that he chooses to abjure direct observation and actual participant accounts does not in any way make his composition more factually accurate. It merely confirms its stature as a great literary composition. But if it is veracity and accuracy of observation we seek, we must go beyond literary composition and linguistic profligacy. Therefore it follows that we must seek out actual participants, observers of the events themselves, as well as observe, as many of the events during the course of their occurrence, in order to avoid suffering the same self-doubts as Maharishi Valmiki suffered and indeed, would likely have succumbed to, had it not been for the timely intervention of Lord Brahma. We cannot all be so fortunate as to have Saptarishi Narada as well as Lord Brahma drop by to reassure us that our composition is beyond reproach, therefore we must rely to a far greater extent on empirical evidence.'

There was another period of silence after he finished speaking.

Three of the five gurus sat down again, stroking their beads vigorously and frowning.

Sniffing Guru and Flashing Eyes stared at him in stupefaction.

Finally, Sniffing Guru said, 'Who are you, boy?'

At almost the same time, Flashing Eyes asked, 'Who is your father?' He turned to the rest of the audience. 'Who is the brahmin responsible for this upstart?'

Vishnu's father stood up, face set in a familiar long-suffering expression. 'I am, gurudev.'

'Punditji?' asked one of the seated gurus. He spoke briefly to his four companions who responded with slow nods of recognition. 'A well-respected scholar,' he concluded.

'Be that as it may,' said Flashing Eyes, 'this is unacceptable behaviour. This insolent upstart has dared to insult the sacred reputation of Maharishi Valmiki himself. He must be penalised for this transgression.'

'Penalised!' repeated Sniffing Guru, sniffing several times, 'Severely!'

A figure rose from the far end of the tent. A tall, lean and darkly clad figure. The moment the audience and the gurus became aware of this person, everyone reacted. A hush came over the tent. Eyes were averted and faces downcast as the tall man strode to the front of the tent. The three gurus who had seated themselves stood up again. All five gurus joined their palms together to show respect to the tall man. He stood beside them, looking at Vishnu Gupta. A faint expression of amusement hung on his face.

'A mere boy,' he said. 'No more than six or seven years of age. Yet his mind is far older and wiser than any six or seven-year-old. Not an acolyte. No mere brahmacharya could possess such a vast store of knowledge as well as the audacity and spirit necessary to interpret that knowledge with a questing, probing spirit, daring to go beyond conventional analysis, to offer a fresh, unreserved perspective on a work that countless pundits and gurus have debated for ages. Not merely intelligent and well educated. Far beyond those levels. A genius. A genuine, born genius. Gifted from birth.'

He turned to look witheringly at the five gurus. 'No question of penalisation. Or censure. This is the very quality of brahmin we require in Pataliputra. It is to give a platform to such young questing minds that this conference is being held. We invited the brightest and best minds in the land to come to Pataliputra and debate freely, and this is by far the best and brightest mind I have had the pleasure of encountering in a long while. It hardly matters if it happens to be housed in a six or seven-year-old body. It is our good fortune to have found it today.'

The tall man put his palms together and inclined his head slightly, acknowledging Vishnu, a child in a tent full of erudite grown men. 'Welcome to Pataliputra, young pundit. The Empire of Magadha has need for minds such as yours. Su-swagatam!' said Maha-amatya Rakshasa to little Vishnu Gupta.

11

Vishnu had never been to a palace in his life. Everything was so big and impressive. There were shiny things everywhere, so much gold plating and jewelled insets. High ceilings and vast chambers with hundreds of carved pillars. Polished floors and gleaming cabinets. Brilliant tapestries and enormous paintings. Sculptures of Samrat Mahapadma Nanda and his family members, each carving several times the size of a living person. And the people were all dressed in rich and fancy clothes, some clearly foreigners from other lands across the ocean or beyond the great Himalayan ranges, wearing the beautifully exotic garments and speaking foreign languages. Even the children were dressed to the nines, standing or walking stiffly as if posing for portraits, none of them laughing, crying or playing. He had never seen so much luxury and so many wealthy, powerful and exotic people in one place before. His mind catalogued and made annotations on a 100 different details, storing each one in its own nook in his limitless brain, compiling a long list of questions about things to look up, ask about, or simply find out more about later.

His father was accompanying him and seemed nervous. Pundit Gupta had a tendency to rub his fingers against his palm briskly when he was nervous. It was an unconscious gesture, something he did without even being aware he was doing it. Vishnu had learned that everybody had a nervous tic or action they repeated when nervous; you only had to be observant enough to notice it. His mother had a tendency to keep rubbing at her left temple, as if pushing back loose hairs, even when her hair was neatly pulled and tied behind her head and there were no loose hairs left to push back. Menaka would frown and squint in a certain way. His second eldest sister Iravati would chew her lower lip. His third eldest sister would screw up her face and hold her breath as if she was about to burst into tears—she was still a baby in some ways, even though she was older than him. It occurred to him then, as he walked through seemingly endless corridors with his father, that he too must have a nervous tic. What was it? He frowned. He would have to note it when he was nervous next.

Right now, he was anxious more than nervous. Anxious to make a good impression on the very important person they were going to see. It was important to his father that they make a good impression, and that made it important to Vishnu as well.

Few people paid any heed to them. The simplicity of their garb and their shaved heads with the single pigtails marked them out clearly as brahmins. There were tens of thousands of brahmins in the city for the conference. Even in the palace complex, Vishnu had seen a huge number. The palace brahmins were distinct from the visitors who came to attend the conference: palace brahmins dressed in red ochre and had a look about them that was sterner, more intense. Many of them looked angry, and were stronger and more muscular looking than their village and town counterparts. They passed a few standing in alcoves, arguing fiercely about something, and to Vishnu it appeared as if these men were on the verge of violence. He dismissed these impressions, thinking that surely brahmins could not act aggressively. No doubt they were merely upset over something and would retreat to meditate and calm themselves. There was a sense of imminent violence in many faces, especially the palace guards and soldiers who were everywhere. As they reached the royal court, he saw several citizens, many visibly poor and ill dressed, standing in a group to one side behind a continuous line of soldiers with spears held sideways, fencing in the citizens. The contrast between their shabby state and the opulence of the setting produced peculiar emotions in his heart. Why were these people here? And why did they look so miserable and shabby? Why were the soldiers guarding them like prisoners? *Were* they prisoners? No, they could not be, because there were actual prisoners over there in the far corner, heavy chains hanging from their wrists and cuffed around their ankles, guarded by soldiers who held their spears pointed *at* the prisoners. One of them was bleeding from a wound that appeared to have been caused by the repeated poking of a spear into his side. Despite the wound and the blood trickling down his thigh, the man still kept shuffling forward, staring sightlessly and mumbling something incoherent. As Vishnu and his father approached the court entrance and slowed, he saw the nearest soldier prod the blind man again.

Vishnu's father scanned the space outside the court. He turned to Vishnu. 'Stay here. I will make enquiries and be back in a moment.'

His father went off in search of someone to speak to as Vishnu drifted a little closer to the prisoners. He was curious to know more about them. What crimes had they committed? Why was that blind man in chains? What had he done that was so terrible that he had to be put in chains? He was blind and clearly old; he could hardly be expected to run away. What was the point in chaining him up?

As he watched, the blind man shuffled forward another step or two again.

Once again, a soldier prodded him with his spear. Vishnu saw the tip of the spear draw blood from the old man's side and winced. If Vishnu had one weakness, it was that he could not stomach blood or violence.

'Stay back, cripple, or the next time I'll drive this spear through and through,' the soldier said curtly.

'Do it. Save the court the time. All these fools are a waste of time anyway.' This came from the next soldier.

'They're all going to die within the hour anyway,' said a third soldier. 'Nobody accused of anything ever leaves here alive.'

The blind man turned his head each time a soldier spoke. After the third soldier made his comment, the blind prisoner said, 'But I'm not a criminal! I'm the victim. Those men came into my house and robbed me. I only came to bear witness against them in court.'

'Witness!' One of the soldiers laughed. 'Blind man pretending to be a witness! That's rich!'

'I heard them speaking to one another. I heard them speak their names, and the name of the crooked merchant to whom they sell their stolen goods. If I hear them speak even once in court, I will be able to identify each one by name. Please, I beg you again, let me speak to the Maha-amatya! He is the Minister of Justice as well as Prime Minister. If you will not allow me, then you go and explain it to him.'

Another soldier laughed. 'The Maha-amatya isn't bothered about your problems. If you don't want to be robbed, hire bodyguards to protect your house.'

'I am an honest citizen,' the blind man said, 'I pay my taxes on time, I have never caused any trouble. My two sons fought and died as soldiers for the Emperor, soldiers just like you. I myself fought as a soldier till I suffered the injury that cost me my sight. What were we fighting for, if not our great empire?'

One of the soldiers quipped: 'You fought for the salary and the chance to loot and rape. With three soldiers in the family, you must have brought in a nice pile of plunder.'

The old man turned his head, looking bewildered by these comments. 'But the city guard is supposed to protect its citizens! Why else do we pay taxes?'

One of the other prisoners, a younger man with a fresh bruise on his cheek from being struck by a guard, put his hand gently on the blind man's shoulder, 'Leave it be, old-timer. These men don't care about us. We are all honest citizens here, come to complain about crimes committed against us or our families. My wife was assaulted and killed in our very home, our daughter taken by the same men to be sold to the slavers. Yet when I came to lodge my complaint, it was I they put in chains.'

'Aye,' said another man bitterly. 'There is no justice in Magadha. The Shishunagas were bad, the Nandas are worse. We are fools to even live in Pataliputra.'

'Meanwhile, the Crown Prince commits all manner of heinous crimes in the palace itself and nothing is done to bring him to justice!' cried out another elderly man. 'My daughters and sons worked for him as personal servants and it is months since they came home. I know they were killed in one of his debauched orgies. Justice is blind in Pataliputra. And the reason lies with that evil man himself, Rakshasa!'

At the mention of this word, the guards lost all their humour. The mocking grins disappeared from their faces. Three of them surged forward as one and together they drove their spears into the body of the old man who had spoken aloud. He cried out as blood spurted from his wounds, and sank to the floor, dying. Still, the soldiers continued stabbing him with their spears until he was little more than a butchered beast.

All the other prisoners had drawn back, away from the old man's body. It lay twitching and haemorrhaging blood from a dozen wounds for several moments. Vishnu watched as the old blind man tilted his head, listening to the sounds, recognising them for what they were. When one of the guards brushed past him, he grabbed hold of the man's throat and began squeezing tightly. The old man was strong, strong enough that the guard was taken unawares and dropped his spear. The other guards' view of this was blocked by the other prisoners, who were standing silently, looking down, avoiding the eyes of the guards as well as ignoring the old blind man. The guards drew together briefly to confer and one of them went striding across the polished floor.

Vishnu was the only one actually in a position to see the old blind man throttling the guard. He noticed the way the other prisoners shuffled closer together, ostensibly to get further away from the bleeding corpse of the other man, but in the process, they also blocked the view of the blind man from the other guards.

He watched with morbid fascination.

The guard had stopped struggling and was now hanging limply in the blind man's hands. The blind man's hands were large enough that his fingers touched and overlapped the guard's throat. He slowly released his grip, revealing the throat he had just crushed.

Vishnu stared, unable to look away, as the blind man let the guard's body fall to the floor. The sound of the guard's head striking the marble floor was loud and sickening. It finally attracted the attention of the other guards. They used their spears to push aside the huddled prisoners and saw their dead companion. One of them handed his spear to someone else and bent down to examine the dead guard.

He stood up looking at the blind man. 'Now you've done it, old man. You've gone and murdered an imperial guard. Do you know the penalty for that?'

The blind man said nothing.

'It's murder, you old fool!' the guard said. He looked around for his spear. 'I should just run you through right here and now for that.'

The blind man raised his head and spread his arms. 'Go ahead.'

The guard stared at him. The blind man remained standing with his arms spread.

'Go ahead,' the blind man repeated. 'Kill me. That is what lies in store for me anyway, is it not? I did not want to believe what everyone said about justice in Magadha but now I know. I no longer wish to live and continue to pay taxes to an unjust regime. Better that I die this very day. Because to support oppression and tyranny is to enable it. I have lived a long and adventurous life. I have fought, travelled and seen the world. I raised a family, all of whom are gone now. I have no one left to live for. Why should I continue living and supporting an evil empire? Kill me now!'

The guard stared at him with a strange expression. Then he backed away slowly. 'The man is insane.'

'Mad as an elephant in masth,' said the guard who had argued with the blind man earlier.

'Shall we run him through as well?' asked another guard.

'No, he killed an imperial guard, he must be brought before Maha-amatya.'

'You're a fool, blind man,' said the first guard. 'You were

only going to be questioned and then let go. Now, it's the kosaghar for you.'

'Not even the kosaghar. I bet you Maha-amatya will give him to Dharma.'

'I'll take that bet,' said another guard, tapping his spear against the other guard's spear. 'Bet you two coppers to one he gets the kosaghar.'

'I'll bet two to one he gets the elephant.'

All the guards then began to place their bets on one of the two options.

Vishnu felt as if he was going to be sick. His feet began carrying him away from the prisoners and guards before he knew he was walking. He had no thoughts or intention, he was simply walking to get away from that horrible place. Two men had died in front of him within moments, for meaningless, pointless reasons. He had never seen a single death with his own eyes before in his life; now he had witnessed two in the same day.

He tried to make sense of things.

12

'Vishnu!'

He turned to see his father hurrying toward him. He stood and waited for him to catch up with him, still feeling numb and unable to identify the precise emotions surging through his being.

'Son, where are you going? We have an important audience today. I told you to wait there for me.'

Vishnu frowned. 'I—'

He was about to say, 'I am here, waiting where you told me.' But he suddenly realised that he was standing on green grass, in the open air, sun shining down on him. He blinked and looked around at the busy people rushing into or out of the palace. He was standing on the front lawn of the main palace where the Emperor's court was housed, in the large quadrangle in the centre of the palace complex. He had no recollection of walking down the stairs and going outside. His feet had carried him of their own volition.

'Are you all right?' his father asked, bending down to look closely at his face. 'You look…upset. Did someone say something to you?'

Vishnu shook his head silently.

His father continued to stare. 'Are you well now? Well

enough to come back inside? The aide told me we would be called in shortly. But if you are not feeling well enough, we can go back to the quarters.'

Vishnu knew how important this audience was for his father's career. A part of him wanted to say, 'Yes, please, let's go back, let's go back home, to our village.' He knew if he said that, his father would take him home without question. At least back to the quarters where he and Vishnu's mother would sit with him and try to understand what had happened to him suddenly. If they did that, he would have to tell them what he had seen and he could not bear to even think about it right now, let alone speak about it. It was...unspeakable. And if he did tell them, his father would no longer want to stay and work in Pataliputra a single day. He would do exactly what Vishnu had suggested and take the family back home to Chanak. And he would spend all his life struggling to eke out a living instead of rising to his full potential and enjoying the opportunities that working in a big city brought.

They had talked about all this, his father and mother, and Vishnu had heard them and understood how important this visit and now this audience was to his father, to their whole family. This was why they had all accompanied him to the conference; because he hoped to secure work here in the capital and if that happened, he wanted his family to be with him. All these thoughts ran through Vishnu's mind in the moments his father stayed bent over, staring at him with curiosity and gentle concern.

'No,' he said at last, 'no, I am well. Let us go inside. I'm sorry I left.'

'That's all right,' his father said kindly. He continued to look at Vishnu. 'Are you sure you are well enough to go through with the audience?'

Vishnu nodded vigorously. He reached out and touched his father's cheek. 'Yes, yes, father. Come, let us go. We must not keep important people waiting.'

His father smiled, and Vishnu felt the cheek moving under his palm. 'Yes, yes, of course. We must never keep important people waiting.'

He straightened up and offered his hand. Vishnu took it, startled at how warm his father's hand was before he realised that it was his hand that was cold. His entire body had gone cold, even though he had been standing out in the sun. He felt as if he had suffered a great shock, but the kindness of his father's face and voice, the strength of his hand, and the awareness of the importance of this day to their family helped Vishnu overcome all the emotions churning inside him.

They walked slowly up the stairs together, into the palace.

13

The court was grander than anything Vishnu had ever seen but he had no eyes for grandeur anymore. All this grandeur, the luxury, the pomp and ceremony, the bright uniforms, the rich apparel, the fine nobles and courtiers, the exotic ambassadors from foreign lands, all of it seemed tawdry and irrelevant to him. The things he had witnessed outside the court had challenged his perception of Pataliputra. He had always assumed that Pataliputra was a place of knowledge and wisdom, justice and peace. He was still coming to terms with reality. His mind still couldn't accept that the truth was so different from the perception. Perhaps that had been an aberration; perhaps those men were not representative of the population, perhaps the guards were over-zealous in their duties, perhaps, perhaps, perhaps... He was still willing to give the great centre of the Magadha Empire the benefit of the doubt. He had to give it the benefit of the doubt because how else could he support his father coming here to work for this same empire, this same city? No, surely those events and sights had been an aberration. Surely the Maha-amatya could not be all that they said he was. What was the word that the prisoner had used? Rakshasa? Rakshasa were evil ruthless monsters. Surely the Prime Minister of Magadha, the Justice

Minister of this greatest civilization, could not be a monster! It was absurd. A lie. Those men were mad. The guards ought not to have killed that prisoner so cruelly right there in the palace, but perhaps they had no choice.

He was only a boy after all, and never before had he been made so aware of this fact. Only a boy. What did he really know about law, ministers, great cities and how they were governed? Only what his father and teacher had told him. He must have misread the situation, misheard the words somehow. He had never misread or misheard anything before in his life, but perhaps it had happened this time. Perhaps, perhaps, perhaps.

It is with such tiny adjustments that we normalise evil, allow tyranny to make its house within our democratic minds, permit the erosion of freedom and justice by those who would warp and bend it to serve their own ends. The intelligent mind questions and doubts everything; devious oppressors know this and use it to force us to question even the most stark facts. Whom will you believe, the tyrant asks, me, or your own lying eyes and senses?

Vishnu Gupta was but a child. An intelligent child. He doubted the evidence of his senses. Had that been the end of it, he would have put aside these doubts and over time accepted them as the aberration he thought they were. One or two incidents can be overlooked, suppressed.

But the day had more shocks and surprises in store for him. History has a way of reminding us when we forget; its lessons are cruel but instructive.

After listening to several incomprehensible discussions about property disputes with long elaborate histories and much back and forth between both sides, each of whom was a richly clad nobleperson from a High House, the court called up 'matters for immediate disposal'.

The prisoners he had seen outside were brought forward, their chains clattering and clanging. The well-dressed courtiers moved to put even more distance from these undesirables.

Maha-amatya, seated on his high seat on his own separate dais, below only the Emperor's own dais, gestured to one of his many aides.

'What are the charges against these prisoners?' asked the aide.

One of the guards who had been watching the prisoners outside came forward hesitantly. 'Treason,' he said simply.

The aide looked at Maha-amatya who nodded slightly.

'And you witnessed the crime?'

The man glanced at the other guards, none of whom spoke or even looked up. They were all busy contemplating the shafts of their spears or the polished blackstone floor. 'Aye,' he said.

The aide looked at Maha-amatya again.

Maha-amatya gestured to the aide.

The aide said aloud: 'The sentence for treason is death by execution, to be carried out at once.'

Someone laughed in the court.

The aide stiffened. He looked around.

The laughter grew until the entire court was silent. Everyone began looking around to identify the source.

It was the blind old man. The one who had strangled the guard who had killed the other prisoner with his spear. He was laughing loudly, irrepressibly.

'You!' shouted the aide, 'Silence! Show respect for the court and the Maha-amatya!'

The guards looked at the blind old man and prodded him with their spears, reopening his earlier wounds, which began to bleed again. Still, the old man continued to laugh.

'SILENCE!' shouted the aide again.

The blind old man suddenly broke off in mid-laugh, resulting in dead silence. Vishnu felt as if he could hear his own heart beating in his chest.

'Justice,' said the blind prisoner.

He stepped forward, ignoring the spears prodding him. He held up his manacled wrists, making his chains clatter. The guards prodding him backed away at once. 'Justice! I demand justice!'

The aide stepped forward, his face already red with anger, and was about to shout again, when the Maha-amatya spoke from his seat.

'Let the prisoner speak.'

The aide turned back in surprise, looked at the Maha-amatya as if making sure that it was he who had spoken. Then quickly recovered his senses and turned back. 'You may speak,' he said stiffly to the blind prisoner. 'But show respect and be brief.'

The blind prisoner grinned, showing his broken and missing teeth. 'Brief is all I have left of life. I lived my life in service to the Empire, my two sons, my family, we all did our part, paid our taxes, did everything right and honest all our lives. My sons gave their lives fighting for you, Samrat Mahapadma Nanda, fighting for what I thought was a great empire. I would often hear tales of excesses, of corruption, of misuse of power, of injustices, but I always argued that some exceptions did not make the rule. I always tried to argue for the empire, because I believed that to build a great empire, you must accept a few sacrifices, a few weaknesses. One does not throw out the entire fruit simply because of a single bruise. One cuts away the bruised portion and eats the rest. For years I ignored the signs, the indications that Magadha only pretended to be a great empire ruled by dharma and justice, that under all the pomp and show was a dark underside, was a tyranny worse than even the Shishunagas at their most corrupt. I forced myself to ignore these indications and continued to believe in the great dream of Magadha despite all these…'

'Come to the point,' Maha-amatya said, 'Unless it is public office you wish to stand for, in which case, you should have presented yourself as a politician, not a prisoner.'

Laughter erupted from the court. People nodded and jeered at the blind man. Vishnu Gupta frowned.

The blind man turned his head, listening to the Maha-amatya's voice, then to the jeering and the laughter.

'I came here to complain of a burglary. Thieves broke into my house and stole all my valuables. I heard their voices and their names and could identify the men responsible. But when I came to report this to the city guard, what do I hear? Those same voices, those very men, the thieves, right there in the city guard's station! When I accused them of robbing me and attempted to report them to their superior, I was put into these chains, and sent here as a prisoner myself. Is this justice?'

Maha-amatya looked at his aide and made a sign. The aide nodded and said aloud: 'The report from the city guard says that you levied a false charge against the Emperor's city guard. The sergeant of the guard station says that you have no proof that any theft occurred at your residence.'

'Proof? My word is my proof. Why else did I go to complain about the burglary? Every last valuable I owned was taken by those men. The very men of the city guard who were supposed to protect me, to protect all of us citizens. At my age, I have no means of supporting myself. That little coin I possessed, those items, they were all that I had to sustain myself in my last years. My beloved wife died years ago in an accident on the city streets, run over by a noble's horse. I accepted it as an accident at that time, even though the noble could have stopped in time. But this robbery happened and I could identify the thieves! At the very least, those men should have been searched and questioned.'

'Your accusations were treasonous. To accuse anyone who serves the Emperor is to accuse the Emperor himself.'

'But what if they are thieves?' asked the blind man. 'Does that make the Emperor also a thief?'

A murmur of consternation rippled through the court.

'You are now making further treasonous remarks,' said the aide, 'this will not be tolerated.'

'I know why those men were not charged. Because the sergeant of the station was himself in league with them. It is a regular occurrence. The guards steal from the people, and pay a portion up the line to their superiors and their superiors in turn, until finally some part of their ill-gotten gains probably reaches even the high halls of this court and the Maha-amatya's office for all we know. How else could this be permitted to happen?'

'Enough!' the aide said. 'This is the babbling of a madman. In addition to your other charges, you are also accused of killing a guard with your bare hands. Do you deny this charge?'

The blind man raised his hands. 'I am proud of that act. For a moment, as I throttled the man's life, I felt that I had gained some small measure of justice. For when tyrants oppress, what choice do ordinary people have but to take the law into their own hands?'

'So in addition to treason, you are also a murderer,' the aide said, ignoring the blind man's other statements. 'The court will now pronounce the means of your execution.'

Maha-amatya rose slowly from his seat, raising his right hand straight out, pointing at the blind prisoner. 'In the name of Samrat Mahapadma Nanda, I declare upon this offender the danda...'

'Dharma.'

Maha-amatya stopped and looked at the prisoner.

'Dharma,' the blind man repeated. 'I ask that I be given the chance to throw myself upon the judgement of Dharma.'

The aide stepped forward angrily, 'You have no right to demand anything! How dare you interrupt the Maha-amatya! The charge for that too is death!'

Maha-amatya gestured at the aide. 'Very well. If the prisoner wishes to opt for the judgement of Dharma, I do not object. All those who come before the court of Samrat Mahapadma Nanda have the right to ask for this option. Let Dharma be brought forward and judge this man's fate himself.'

A wave of excited whispers passed through the court. Vishnu saw several people move aside quickly, glancing back over their shoulders as if fearing a great calamity.

A trumpeting sound echoed through the many pillared hall, making many gasp in terror. Several of the men and the women looked nervous.

The biggest and blackest elephant Vishnu had ever seen was brought forward, held by a long heavy chain through the most tender part of his mouth. The man who led him was a huge, muscular giant himself, towering above even the tallest guards. He lumbered through the court, pulling the elephant behind him like a goat on a tether. The elephant's eyes were dark and filled with a dark fury. His mouth was awash with white foam and his hide was scored with several cuts and marks as if he had been prodded and cut like the prisoners by the guards. He kept trying to raise his trunk to lash out at his captor but the chain, wound around his trunk as well, prevented him. The pull on his soft mouth forced him to follow.

The mahout brought the elephant to a spot where a large stone block rested on the floor of the court hall. Vishnu had noticed it when he entered and took it to be a bench. But he saw now that it had a small depression in the middle of the seat and was too narrow to be a comfortable bench.

The guards took hold of the blind man's chains and dragged him forward. He stumbled and was forced to his knees. The guards forced his head on to the stone block and placed his neck in the depression. It cradled the man's skull neatly, leaving more than half the head above the level of the stone itself.

The mahout compelled the elephant forward with forceful actions and gestures. At this point, the elephant seemed to know what to do; he allowed himself to be brought close enough to raise his foot above the head of the blind prisoner. The mahout used the chains to force the elephant to stand in that pose for a moment.

'Dharma!' asked the Maha-amatya, using a deeper, more resonant voice that rebounded throughout the hall. 'Guilty or not guilty?'

The elephant's eyes rolled wildly, and he trumpeted through his chained mouth and trunk. The sound was deafening, making Vishnu want to cringe and cover his ears.

Then the elephant brought his foot down with an impact that he felt through the soles of his feet, in his very bones, producing a second, much more terrible sound.

Vishnu felt as if his heart shuddered and stopped beating at the reverberation from that impact.

Maha-amatya raised both his hands. 'Dharma has pronounced judgement. His verdict is Guilty. Let this be a reminder to all those who challenge the supremacy of the Nanda dynasty. We are ruled by Dharma and those who oppose us, are against Dharma. As even our most ancient scriptures tell us, in the battle between Dharma and Adharma, Dharma always wins. Let this be a lesson to all.'

14

'Ah, the young scholar. I am pleased you were on hand to witness the danda. Justice is an integral part of governance. It is the backbone of our functioning. Without justice, there can be no society, no kingdom, no empire.'

Vishnu was silent. His father glanced at him, then filled the silence, 'It was an honour to attend your court, Maha-amatya.' He glanced again at Vishnu, who remained silent. 'Vishnu and I are both grateful for the great opportunity. He was most excited to come here today. It is a momentous occasion.'

Maha-amatya glanced down at the boy. They were in his private chamber where they had been brought by one of his many aides after the conclusion of the day's court hearings. 'He does not seem as excited now. Or has he lost his voice?'

His father looked at him yet again. 'He was feeling poorly; I think the excitement and exertion of the big day has worn him down. He is, after all, still young.'

'But a brilliant one,' Maha-amatya said, 'and brilliant minds are always welcome at Pataliputra. You yourself have a fine reputation as a scholar, Pundit Gupta. But you have outdone yourself with your son's education. I meet countless brahmins daily, they pass through my city like water through the Ganga's banks. I have met some rare specimens who are gifted with genius at a very young age, and many more who are gifted with great wisdom and insight after a lifetime of learning and study. But never before have I met a brahmin who has both genius and wisdom at such a tender age. Truly, your son is a prodigy.'

'You are too kind, gurudev. I thank you.'

'Don't thank me yet. I have yet to speak of the reason why I summoned you both here today.'

Maha-amatya then explained his plan for a centre of learning and study for scholars from across the empire. 'And foreign lands as well. For the great ocean of knowledge touches all shores.'

A centre that would be the single largest gathering of intellectuals and thinkers. It would be like the conference currently being held in the capital city, but instead of a few weeks, it would continue all year round, indefinitely.

The goal, Maha-amatya said, was to create a caucus of learning with no rival in the world. It had been his dream for years but only now, with the empire stable and relatively at peace, was he in a position to finally implement his grand dream.

'It is a great vision,' Pundit Gupta said at last, when the Prime Minister had finished. 'A magnificent vision. It would be my great honour to be a part of this venture.'

'Both of you,' Maha-amatya said. 'My offer is extended to yourself as well as your son.'

Both of them looked at Vishnu Gupta.

Vishnu's father cleared his throat. He was not the sort of father who nudged or used physical coercion to prod his children at any time. But his eagerness to consummate this opportunity was palpable in his face and manner. For his sake, Vishnu finally broke the silence that had sealed his lips for the past few hours and spoke at last.

'My father speaks for us both,' he said.

They both waited.

Vishnu said nothing further.

Maha-amatya frowned. 'The boy I heard in the conference that day did not lack words to express himself. What is the cause of this sudden reticence?'

'Maha-amatyaji, forgive my son. As I said, he is merely tired and a little unwell. A good night's rest will revive him. I assure you he is as enthusiastic and eager to accept your offer as am I. As he said, I express on both our behalf our great appreciation for your generous offer.'

'Leave us,' Maha-amatya said.

Pundit Gupta stared.

'I wish to have words with the young pundit alone,' Maha-amatya said. 'It will not take more than a few moments. Please wait outside.'

Vishnu saw his father look uncertainly at him and nodded once. Pundit Gupta was reassured by his son's response, but still looked uncomfortable. He left with more than one glance back over his shoulder. The aide that showed him out of the Maha-amatya's chamber shut the door behind himself.

Now, Maha-amatya and Vishnu were alone together.

15

He towered about Vishnu like a tree before a sapling. His dark garb and heavy rudraksh mala—it was believed to have 1,008 beads—made him seem even taller and leaner. His long hatchet face with the hooked nose and dark, deeply set eyes stared down at Vishnu intently. A long moment of silence passed during which neither boy nor man said a word.

Maha-amatya allowed himself a faint twitch. Perhaps that was what passed for a smile on his face. Perhaps it was merely a twitch.

'Something troubles you, young one. What is it?'

Vishnu said nothing. Even at his tender age, he had learned already that at times the best response was a lack of response. Many mistook a lack of response to be *no* response: that was not true. When someone wanted you to answer a question and you remained silent, you were in effect refusing to answer. Silence became a form of resistance.

Another long silence ensued.

Maha-amatya nodded very slightly, barely a movement. 'You saw something. Heard something. Whatever it was, it changed your opinion of me. Or perhaps you had no opinion and now you do. Be that as it may, it does not change the facts. Do you know what the facts are, young pundit?'

Vishnu remained silent.

'I possess the power to ruin your life, your family's life, your loved ones, with a single gesture. Not even an order or a writ. Merely a gesture.'

Maha-amatya made a gesture, moving his fingers in one of the actions Vishnu had seen him use earlier in court, when sentencing the blind man.

'That is all it would take. And you, and your family, would be eliminated. You would cease to exist. It would be as if you never were, and will never be. No trace will remain of your time upon this mortal plane.'

He watched Vishnu Gupta, waiting for some reaction. When none came, he said, 'Is that what you wish?'

Vishnu still did not reply.

'On the other hand, I could hire your father for the post I offered him. As a professor, he would teach advanced classes in his specialised areas of knowledge, and in time, as the institute expands, he would be a guru to other gurus. It would be a great prestige and honour for him as he would be under the aegis of Magadha and the Emperor himself. He would receive comfortable housing for his entire family, a good income which he would never need to spend because all his family's needs would be taken care of by the empire, and he would be elevated above other brahmins, gurus and pundits, part of my personal host of brahmins. His future would be secure, your sisters would find excellent husbands, you would be heir to a considerable fortune and lifelong income, and in time, your family would be endowed with lands and property, as well as slaves to service them. You could be an aristocrat, a noble, a minister, even perhaps a Maha-amatya like myself someday. There will be no limit to your achievements and success. And it would all begin today, this very minute, changing your life forever.'

Vishnu's face remained impassive, revealing nothing, his lips speaking no words.

'Perhaps you are thinking that you will continue to remain silent, no matter what I say. That I will lose patience and dismiss you, and your father and your family and you yourself will return home to your little village wherever it might be, to your simple, rustic life. I am sure until you came here to Pataliputra you considered it a good enough life and were expecting to spend the rest of your life peacefully there. You may well feel that it is better to enjoy the simple pleasures of existence there, rather than enter the tumultous and frightening challenge of living and working in the big city, dealing with the complex politics of the empire. You may believe that in days you will put this visit behind you and resume your life as it was. However, I am now informing you that this will never happen. You will either leave after accepting my offer, or you will never leave here alive. Whatever life you had until you came here, that life is now gone. Whatever you thought you enjoyed or experienced is over. Now begins your new life—or not, as you wish. In either case, your old life is over. That Gupta family is now dead and cremated. You can never go home again. I have already executed that former version of you. There is now only my way, or no way at all.'

Vishnu heard this whole argument out without response, then waited a further moment before saying a single word: 'Why?'

Maha-amatya's cheek muscle twitched again in that ghost of a smile. 'Good. Finally you engage with me. I knew you could not remain silent. You are not one of those who suffers in silence and endures. You are a fighter, and fighters always engage, no matter the odds or their own condition. Despite being born into the brahmin varna, you are at heart a warrior, a kshatriya, perhaps even one with the potential to become a yoddha someday, a master warrior. You will fight and die fighting, but never stand by silently. I knew this, and you have proved me correct.'

Vishnu stood silent, expectant.

Maha-amatya nodded again, the slightest of nods. A mere tilt of his bony avian head. A vulture dipping its beak into the fresh carcass of its meal. 'Why, you ask. The perfect question. I shall give you the perfect answer.'

He gestured at the chamber around himself, austere and sparse compared to the rest of the palace that Vishnu had seen so far, but still opulent in its polished floors, high ceilings, carved pillars, friezes and statuary, art and tapestries. There was more wealth displayed in the architecture and furnishings of that chamber than the entire population of Vishnu's entire village of Chanak had possessed in their lifetime.

'This,' he said, 'this power I wield. It did not simply *come* to me. Power is not a dog that comes wagging its tail when you whistle. It is a wolf that snarls and is powerful enough to rip your throat out with a single action. It cannot be domesticated; it must be conquered. And to conquer the wolf of power, one must use hard steel and even harder resolve.'

Maha-amatya tapped his head. 'Our greatest weapon is here. The mind. The flesh is weak; blades rend it, claws and teeth and almost any sharp object can penetrate it and kill our bodies. But with the power of the mind, one can subjugate other people, all people; slaughter thousands, tens of thousands, even crores if one wills it. Or enslave and put them to work. Empires are built not only with brute force, though that is essential, but with brute will. One must be able to outwit and outthink the enemy at all times. It is an advantage that can overcome almost any deficiency: superior numbers, strategic position, embattlements. Whatever the enemy's advantage, if you can think of a way to overcome it, you can achieve it. There may be times when your armies cannot execute your orders perfectly and you will fail occasionally. But if you cannot think of a way to succeed, you will always fail.'

He gestured in the direction they had come from, the direction of the court. 'Kings, emperors, princes, however strong, virile and brilliant they may be at war and strategy, they are limited by their physicality. Rulers are not bred for genius, but for dominance by force and by the accident of birth. A prince can be born a prince and become a king without having done anything to deserve the title. But a minister cannot rise to prominence simply by being born a minister. There are many who try, and they may find a place in the aristocracy, they may even inveigle their way into a position of power temporarily. But in the long run, they too cannot match the pure brilliance of genius. Genius outshines all other suns; it is the solar power that blazes a trail that none can follow or equal. And when you combine great genius with great power, you have something immutable. The force that can topple empires, or build new ones.'

Maha-amatya gestured at a portrait of Samrat Mahapadma Nanda, sitting on his throne in all his imperial finery, the artist contriving to make even his squat, unremarkable features appear almost handsome. 'Mahapadma was no greater, wiser or better a man than his predecessor. Nor is the Nanda dynasty any better than the Shishunaga dynasty. Both operate much the same way, utilising the same methods to rule, the same mercantile system to profit, the same age-old devices to manipulate the citizenry and lull it into complacency. What brought Mahapadma to power, what brings all brash young hopefuls into power, was the mind behind the coup. My mind. More important than simply coming to power, I designed it so that he would stay in power, and create a dynasty. One that would rule for centuries, perhaps even millennia. And a design of that complexity and brilliance is not simply the work of a single mind. Genius though I am, I am still only as powerful or weak as my resources. I cannot be everywhere at once, nor see, hear and know everything that occurs, or who does what, and when, and why.

'That is why I built a network of geniuses. A brains trust. A collection of the best minds I could find, wherever I could find them. When I see genius, I do not hesitate, I hire it at once. For two reasons: One, that a brilliant mind can be of great value to me if used correctly. Two, if I do not use that mind, someone else may use it against me someday. Genius is a sharp sword. Better I hold it with the hilt in my fist rather than someone else hold it and point the blade at my belly.

'You, young pundit, are a genius. You must already know that. You are exceptionally gifted with intelligence, power of retention, analytical ability, insight, the talent to be able to make creative leaps based on the merest of evidence… All this at age seven. I have made it my life's work to study genius and its uses. I believe you have extraordinary potential.'

He held up a hand, displaying a large lined palm, and impossibly long knobbly fingers. That hand alone would have covered Vishnu's entire scalp, had the Maha-amatya placed it on his head. 'Five. That is the number. Only a handful of other pundits I have encountered have displayed such astonishing talent. I, of course, am foremost among them. Three others are dead; two because they opposed me, one because he came afoul of a political complication that he should have known better than to steer free of. You are the fifth. I may find a sixth in the next decade or two, perhaps even a seventh before I die, but perhaps not. You are here now, and at a ripe young age, suitable for recruitment. Or so I thought.

'After listening to you speak at the conference, and having already heard your father speak on two occasions on previous days, I already know that you are both of a liberal set of mind. You believe in the innate goodness of all living creatures, and that we are here for the purpose of doing good to others. That we are all brothers and sisters, struggling against the same odds and challenges, and it is our moral duty to aid one another whenever possible. You believe in dharma and the exploits of the great heroes. No doubt, you consider Rama Chandra and Krishna, Arjun, and all the other heroic do-gooders to be emblems of nobility. You believe that emperors and kings must rule kindly, wisely, justly, and care for their citizens, and do no harm. You have all these wonderful romantic notions and ideals.'

He paused and looked at Vishnu Gupta. 'This makes you dangerous. A romantic, moral person, one who believes in ideals like dharma and goodness, is a potential threat to me, my emperor, and the security of Magadha. That is why. That is why I cannot let you leave here alive if you refuse to work for me. Because someday, for whatever reason, you may choose to use that mind against me, or my empire, and at that stage, for all I know, you may have joined with a physical power, or been forcibly compelled to work for some power, and your agenda may be antagonistic to my own agenda. And that brilliant genius mind will then be used against me. And as a genius brahmin myself, Vishnu Gupta, I know all too well how such a mind can be a powerful tool if used correctly. It can topple empires and build new ones. It took one brahmin genius, myself, to topple the Shishunagas, and bring the Nandas to power in Magadha. I cannot risk the chance that another such mind could someday pose a threat to all that I have built here. Simpler then to eliminate you here and now, end the potential threat before it even matures. Drown the kitten before it grows up to become a snarling lioness. That is why, Vishnu Gupta.'

Vishnu was silent for another long moment. Maha-amatya watched him and waited calmly, not pressuring him into responding. They stood there for several moments, man and boy, Prime Minister of Magadha and a simple brahmin's son from the tiny backwoods village of Chanak.

Finally, Vishnu spoke.

'I agree to your offer.'

Maha-amatya waited but Vishnu said no more. He had said all that he needed to say.

Maha-amatya permitted himself a slightly more pronounced twitch of his muscular cheek. 'That is good. It would be better to make use of that genius mind you possess than to destroy it. But you understand that this is not merely a posting or an appointment. This is a commitment for life. Your life, your family's lives, and the lives of any descendants of your family. From this moment on, all in your line will serve only me and be loyal solely to me, on pain of death. There is no exception to this rule, no termination clause to this loyalty, no exclusion or condition precedent.'

Vishnu inclined his bald head. 'I understand.'

'Very good,' Maha-amatya said, 'in that case, our business here is done.'

He gestured to the empty room and the doors swung open at once.

Vishnu frowned for the first time, glancing around.

Maha-amatya saw the look. 'Here in Magadha, you are never truly alone. Even the walls have ears and eyes. Remember that, young pundit.'

Vishnu met his new master's eyes once more, then exited the room, walking as briskly as his little feet would carry him.

16

His father looked relieved and happy to see him. He bent down with a smile, looking at Vishnu's face. 'At last!'

Vishnu smiled at his father. 'You have the job, father! You will be head of the new institute! We will all live here in Pataliputra in fine quarters. The Maha-amatya told me himself!'

Pundit Gupta smiled, his eyes lighting up. 'That is wonderful news. I must go see him now to thank him.'

'That will not be necessary, father,' Vishnu said, taking his father's hand. 'He has told me everything already. I will explain it to you as we walk home. But let's start walking now, I am terribly hungry. Rats are chewing at my insides!'

'Very well,' his father said, starting to walk away after one last glance at the doors through which Vishnu had emerged. They had already closed again. 'But I don't understand. You were in there for so long.'

'Talking.'

'Such a long talk! What did the Maha-amatya say to you in there? Why the need for privacy?'

Vishnu shrugged and smiled up at his father. 'He wanted to test my intelligence, a special test he has devised for young geniuses,' he said.

'That sounds quite intriguing,' his father said as they walked down one of many long stairways in the palace complex. 'What sort of questions were there in the test? Knowing your memory, you must recall them all exactly. Tell me every question and how you answered it.'

'It wasn't that kind of test,' Vishnu said as they emerged into the sunlit gardens of the palace. 'It was more of a comprehension exercise. He told me a long story and asked me to give him a yes or no answer. It was something like a riddle with only one correct answer.'

'That is even more intriguing,' his father said, 'What was the story and the question?'

Vishnu grinned up at his father. 'That is the reason for the privacy. He does not wish the details of the test to be known to anyone else. He expressly asked me to respect its confidentiality.'

'Oh.' His father looked disappointed. They walked along in silence for several moments. 'Oh well,' he said at last, 'the point is you were given this great opportunity, and you passed his test.' Pundit Gupta frowned and glanced at his son again. 'That is, you did pass, did you not?'

'Of course, father,' Vishnu said, 'I always pass, you know that.'

From a verandah high up on the upper floors of the palace complex, Maha-amatya watched the quadrangle across which the little boy with the bobbing chotti and his father walked, hand in hand. One of his many aides stood nearby, awaiting his orders.

'They are to be watched,' he said. 'Every member of that family. I wish to know everything they do, however small or seemingly inconsequential. Put our best spasas on the job.'

'As you say, Maha-amatyaji,' said the aide. He paused. 'Should I choose spies used for intelligence gathering, or the ones we use for both spying and assassination?'

'For now, spying is sufficient,' Maha-amatya said, 'the order is only to watch and report.'

The aide nodded and moved aside to pass on the Maha-amatya's instructions to his aide.

The Maha-amatya surveyed his domain.

17

From that day onward, Vishnu lived two lives.

The first life was the same he had been living until then, that of a little scholar. Instead of the village gurukul in Chanak, and his father as a tutor, he now sat with classes of grown men, the most learned pundits and gurus in the empire, mostly only listening at first, but also asking questions, discussing, debating. Because it was known that he was the Maha-amatya's own pet prodigy, no pundit ever denied him anything. All their knowledge was his to access; no question was too bold, no theory too transgressive. He was permitted free access to all topics and schools of study. He dove into the deepest pools of knowledge and emerged refreshed and enriched each time. His mental growth, which was always rapid even in Chanak, now progressed by leaps and bounds; he acquired in months what other scholars took years to learn.

It soon became apparent to all his teachers and fellow scholars that his was a unique mind, capable of intuitive leaps that were uncommon or even unheard of in scholarly circles. While many traditionalists frowned upon such leaps that often seemed to have no basis in rigorous fact, many others argued that it was due to such leaps that great breakthroughs had been accomplished. Such works as the compilation of the Vedas by

Krishna Dweipayana Vyasa, as well as his own composition of the great epic Jaya, itself considered the fifth Veda, had not come about through step-by-step progression; it required a stroke of genius.

Genius. The word came to be bandied about a great deal in the intellectual circles of the empire's capital during those months.

Even the most jealous and egoistic of pundits was forced to acknowledge the innate superiority of Vishnu Gupta's intelligence and his eidetic memory. They might have decades more of study but all that time and effort could not match the ability to simply hear a passage once and recite it back word for word without a single error. Or the ability to compose additional shlokas in the same meter, adding to the original work, with flawless prosody and grammar.

Vishnu's intellectual rigour was incomparable, his hard work unmatched, his application and dedication an inspiration, his insights and leaps a revelation. Soon, even his worst critics became his biggest supporters. He began to win over the intellectuals and pundits one by one, then in entire groups at one time. In mere months since his arrival at Pataliputra, it could be said that he enjoyed the whole-hearted support of the majority of the brahmin caucus in the city, some 5,000 pundits permanently employed by the empire and all under the direct oversight of Maha-amatya Kartikeya himself.

The spies reported back to Maha-amatya on a regular basis, but invariably they had nothing of interest to report. Vishnu Gupta was studying, attending class, debating, discussing... repeat ad infinitum. His family's activities were, of course, equally prosaic, for the first and most vital decision he had taken on that fateful day of his encounter with Maha-amatya, was to never reveal the true nature of the Prime Minister and the Empire to his loved ones. He knew that the day he told them how evil the Maha-amatya was, Rakshasa as he was called by those who knew his true nature, his family would lose all aspiration and hope. They would only want to leave Pataliputra and go home at once. And if they did that, they would all be killed, Vishnu included. If they stayed and attempted to resist or even speak out about Rakshasa's evil ways, they would be killed. If Vishnu himself tried to do anything that could be perceived as resisting or going against the Maha-amatya, they would all be killed.

So he simply continued as if he had never had that conversation, never seen those things that he had seen, never had that glimpse of the evil side of the great empire and its equally great architect. He did what he had always wanted to do all his life: devoted himself to the pursuit of knowledge. He threw himself whole-heartedly into this life and in its own way, it was wonderful. It was everything he had desired and longed for. It was his dream come true, to have all the knowledge of the world at his fingertips, and great minds with whom to discuss and debate it.

But there was a second life that Vishnu lived at the same time.

This was the invisible life he lived, in the privacy of his mindspace.

This was a space even the most observant spasa could not penetrate. No spy could see inside his head, hear his innermost thoughts, or know what he was thinking but never saying.

And inside this mindspace, he built a new self. This was the self that focused on one particular area of knowledge.

Justice.

Nyaya, as it was known in the scriptures.

∞

From the very first day he set foot in the city, Vishnu knew that justice was an absent master in Pataliputra. On the day that he visited the palace and witnessed the horrific injustice, the travesty of a trial, and the brutal execution of what was, in essence, an innocent man driven to desperation, he became aware that injustice wore the garb of justice in this place. Though he had no prior experience of such horrors, Vishnu was no ordinary seven-year-old boy. He knew his scriptures intimately. And what else were the scriptures but a body of knowledge—literally, since the words 'Rig Veda' meant 'Book of Knowledge'—that contained the collective experience and wisdom of humankind.

And as long as humankind has existed, its nemesis has existed as well. Call it asura, call it rakshasa, call it adharma, there has always been an anti-force that countered the force of life itself. Call it anti-life, call it evil, call it whatever one would, it existed, had always existed, and would always exist. It was the reason the great Protector had to take avatar after avatar, rising again in each new age to fight the new avatar of evil.

Every Rama had his Ravana.

Every Sita had her Surpanakha.

Every family of Pandavas had their Kauravas.

Every Kali her Raktasura.

Every force of dharma had an equal opposite force of adharma.

Every unstoppable force had an immovable object.

It was the way of the world. Itihasa was filled with countless examples of such conflicts, of how injustice repeatedly rose again and again, seeking to crush the spirit and hope of humankind, and how justice was forced to take up a sword and do battle.

Despite the shock of viewing those brutal deaths and that shocking injustice, Vishnu did not cry out, protest, argue, complain or react in any way. Because he knew it would do no good.

If a street is already dirty, you are more likely to toss your own refuse there as well. Filth invites filth.

If a street is pristine, you know yours would be the only refuse, and therefore more visible. Even if you are not a good citizen, you would be cautious about throwing refuse because of the risk of being seen by the authorities and penalised or punished for the littering.

Vishnu had known at once that the incidents he witnessed were not exceptions. Those innocent men being treated so brutally were not the first innocent persons treated thus. It was evident from the sheer mundaneness of the incidents, the reactions of the guards, the openly public nature of the treatment, the relative indifference of the court itself, the practiced way the Maha-amatya, his aides, and everyone else participating in that travesty of a 'trial' that this happened routinely, daily. He had picked up many further clues from what he had seen and heard around the city; the incident with his sister Menaka, and other things he had noted with his perpetually observing mind.

And it had all coalesced when the Maha-amatya had delivered that soliloquy on genius and empires. He had been making a single point: That genius was a super-power that could achieve anything it desired, using the right tools, be it an emperor, an army, an assassin, a spy, or even the world's biggest gathering of brahmin intellectuals.

Maha-amatya had chosen to use his genius to build the Nanda dynasty, wresting control of the Magadhan Empire from the Shishunagas by brute force, building not a better empire in its place, but simply his empire.

As Maha-amatya had talked and talked that day, Vishnu Gupta had listened and thought.

By the time he walked out of that chamber that day, he had a single goal in mind: To use his genius to reshape the Magadha Empire into a better Empire. A just Empire. A place where Nyaya was respected and followed.

The first step to doing that was to learn all he could about Nyaya itself.

And what better way could there be to study Nyaya than to observe its opposite, Anyaya, in action!

That was what Vishnu did from that day on.

He observed, watched, heard, overheard, deduced, picked up, noted, and, through a number of means, gathered all the information he could on the injustices being committed within the walls of Pataliputra. He never spoke of these injustices aloud. His goal was not to save that one blind man; he was aware that he could not save that one man or any of the people being treated unjustly today.

All he could do for now was observe and learn. One day his time would come; he would find the means and power to fight injustice with justice. But he would only do that when he was certain that justice would win. Because to lose would cost him not only his own life, but the lives of his entire family. The Maha-amatya had made that crystal clear.

He was playing for high stakes, the highest possible: the lives and well being of his loved ones.

They mattered far more to Vishnu than one innocent prisoner. Or even a thousand innocent men.

Until the time was right, he could not do anything or say anything to risk their lives.

He was young, he had his whole life ahead of him; time was on his side. He would bide his time, continue his education, build his resources, and someday in the future, when the time was right, he would put all his knowledge, his insights, his education, his genius to work. And on that day, justice would triumph over injustice.

He expected that day would take several years. Perhaps even decades. He was content to wait that long. One of the qualities of the essentially good person is fortitude. Rama had endured fourteen long years of exile; the Pandavas had endured more than one exile; Draupadi and Drishyadumna had waited for more than one lifetime to achieve their justice. Vishnu Gupta was willing to wait as long as it took, a decade, or two, or four; it did not matter. His time would come and when it came he would be ready and certain of success.

What he did not count on or expect, was that it would come so soon.

Before he was ready.

Not in decades or even in years.

But mere months later.

18

'Vishnu!'

Vishnu paused in mid-flow. He was discussing the use of meter in shlokas in the Ramayana versus Jaya, and the difference between Valmiki's and Vyasa's use of prosody to suit their respective narrative styles. He looked up to see the last person he would have expected: his eldest sister Menaka was standing outside the window, gesturing frantically. For a moment he wondered why she was at the window instead of coming to the doorway then he recalled the absurd rule that permitted only male brahmins to enter the institute. The room full of brahmins, several of them quite elderly, was glaring at her with disapproval, both because she was interrupting the discussion and also because she was female.

Menaka gestured again to him, silently mouthing 'Come out. Please!' She joined her palms together.

He tendered an apology to the room full of brahmins and left the institute at once. Menaka was not the kind to panic without cause. Whatever had brought her to intrude, it must be urgent and personal.

Menaka came rushing to the entrance as he came out, blinking in the bright sunshine. 'Vishnu, you have to help me. They have arrested him.'

He looked at her. He had rarely seen her this upset, her pretty face wet with tears, her hair in disarray. 'Chandra,' he said.

'Yes!'

He nodded. He knew that Menaka and Chandra had become friends ever since the young man had saved her from being abducted. Perhaps more than just friends. His father and mother were not aware. Perhaps his mother was aware but if so, she had not spoken about it in Vishnu's presence. He was not home that much these days, but he picked up enough clues from the conversations he had with his parents, with Menaka, and most of all, his other two sisters, both of whom were inveterate gossips and could never keep a secret. They both knew of course, but had made a solemn pact to never speak of it openly; which of course led to a great deal of giggling, whispered comments and hand signals, and even some pig Sanskrit, which they thought Vishnu didn't understand but which he understood perfectly well. He had picked up several languages and dialects just by listening to people around him in Pataliputra, but he was very careful not to speak to people in those languages. In this way, he could understand what they were saying in their own language and dialect, but not let on that he understood. He had learned this trick by dealing with his sisters: by pretending to be mystified by their pig Sanskrit chattering, he could learn all the gossip while letting them believe their code was unbreakable.

Menaka and he walked together as she explained what had happened. Chandra had been taken away by the black-garbed palace guards late that morning. As usual when the palace guards arrested someone, there was no information about the reason for the arrest or about where he had been taken. She was in tears and great distress because she knew as well as anyone living in Pataliputra that merely to be arrested was the end. No one who was arrested, for whatever reason, was ever released. No one returned alive. In most cases, no one even knew where they were taken and what happened to them. The few who were openly paraded in court in chains daily were mostly complainants, the victims of the crimes committed every day (and night) in the metropolis. The actual criminals were almost never seen or heard from.

Menaka feared that Chandra's arrest meant she would never see him alive again.

Vishnu agreed with this conclusion. He had learned a great deal about how the city's justice system functioned in these past months. None of it gave him any reason to hope for anything else.

In essence, almost anyone who came in the way of those who enforced the law, be it the city guard, the palace guard, or soldiers, was arrested. In the rare event that the person was someone high ranking, or rich and powerful enough to pay a bribe or exert political influence, they would only be taught a lesson and released. 'Taught a lesson' was a euphemistic way to describe the physical abuse, privation, starvation and incarceration in filthy vermin-infested dungeons in rusty jagged-edged chains and manacles. Almost all of these returned to their families with some form of permanent damage, physical, mental and emotional as well. Many acquired diseases, infections, or severe injuries during the period of incarceration and died after returning home.

Those who had no recourse to political influence or coin for bribes were doomed from the start. They were crushed under the relentless wheels of injustice. A few specimens, randomly cut off from the herd, were paraded in court each day to serve as examples of the rigorously effective law and order of Magadha. The real criminals, those who actually committed the worst, most unspeakable crimes, were rarely apprehended. They survived through a network of weekly bribes passed up the line from the lowliest guard or soldier, through the ranks to the highest officials, all the way up to the Maha-amatya himself. The Prime Minister was never explicitly named or even referred to indirectly, but it was self-evident, since he was both Minister of Justice and Prime Minister, the supreme authority on all matters of law and order in the city.

Vishnu had seen and heard enough to know that the 'Rakshasa' mentioned in whispers was none other than Maha-amatya Kartikeya. Many people did not even know his real name, referring to him only as Maha-amatya, as he had occupied that prime position for as long as they could remember. Though he functioned in the Emperor's name, the reality was that he was an emperor unto himself in all but name. No one dared question his authority, or resist his agenda. To run afoul of him was to risk the destruction of one's entire family.

As for the unfortunates who died in untold numbers every day at the hands of the state—the numbers varied from dozens to hundreds daily, depending on whom one believed—their bodies were piled in a mass cremation each evening in the burning ghats behind the city. The wind usually blew from the south west in the evenings in Pataliputra, passing from the cremation ghats over the poorest areas of the Lower City. Vishnu had never actually visited that crime-ridden, disease-riddled miserably impoverished quadrant but he had heard that each evening, as the mass pyres burned, the ash drifted and settled over the Ashpile—as the poorest sector was nicknamed. A permanent layer of grey ash and grime lay over everything there as a result.

Now, Chandra was gone. At least Menaka had witnessed the apprehension so she knew for certain that he had been taken by the palace guard because of their black uniforms and the Emperor's emblem. That was good to know, but not of much help otherwise. Had it been the city guard, there was still a possibility of bribes. Remote and unlikely, but possible. But with the palace guard, even bribes were not enough. Political influence with enough money to sway those higher up the line of corruption could perhaps make some difference, but Vishnu's family did not have that kind of wealth or influence.

Certainly, he had some access to the Maha-amatya. But access was not the same as influence as many an unfortunate brahmin had learned to his detriment during these past months alone. From time to time some rishi or sadhu would boast that he knew the Maha-amatya and could make this or that happen. This usually happened to brahmins who consumed intoxicating drinks or foods, against their vows, and got into fights or disagreements with other non-brahmins. Such threats were a grave error. These brahmins would invariably receive a curt dismissal from the institute and from Pataliputra on orders of the Maha-amatya himself, conveyed as always by the palace guards. This amounted to a lifelong exile from the capital city, which effectively ended that brahmin's career. Only two such fools had made this mistake during Vishnu's stay here, although apocryphal stories about other foolhardy cases were constantly mentioned as cautionary tales.

The only reason they were exiled rather than 'taught a lesson' or executed summarily was because they were brahmins.

Not only was Chandra not a brahmin, he didn't even know what varna he belonged to. He was an abandoned child, deposited at birth by unknown hands outside an ashram in a small town along with a female baby. It was assumed that the girl was his sister; Chandra grew up regarding her as his sister, the only family he ever had. They had loved and cared for each other during their childhood and pubescent years. When she was taken by visiting 'recruitment agents' who passed through small towns in search of attractive young boys and girls, he was devastated. He had been brought up until then to respect laws and rules, and was a perfectly behaved young boy. But after his sister's abduction, and as he came to learn what happened to such victims, the kind of abuse they were subjected to during their short tortuous lives, he broke away from his earlier self completely. That was the start of his life as a petty criminal, pickpocketing his way from town to town, hoping someday to see his sister or at least find out what had happened to her. His dreams of someday seeing her again were dashed to bits when he entered Pataliputra and was caught in the net of the 'great' city.

Vishnu had spent hours with Chandra, asking pointed questions and learning a great deal about the inner workings of the nexus between the criminal underworld and the political overworld that encouraged, managed, and profited from it. One could not function without the other. That was where true political power and wealth was accumulated. The irony that the same persons who were ostensibly appointed to care for the welfare of citizens were also the ones who preyed on them was lost on most people, who lived in the naive notion that criminals and politicians were two separate species. Even the term 'underworld' implied that there was another invisible secret layer beneath the visible city.

Chandra had smashed this illusion, showing Vishnu how to spot and identify the criminals in their midst, thieves, burglars, rapists, murderers, thugs-for-hire, smugglers, kidnappers, all living alternate lives as seemingly ordinary citizens, going about their lives in the same way that shopkeepers, grocers, farmers, traders, merchants, moneylenders, pundits, fruit sellers, carters, and other people did. They shopped in the same markets, wore more or less the same clothes for the most part, looked almost the same. They just also happened to break skulls and bones, steal coin and valuables, assault and batter, murder and maim. There was no underworld buried below the city. It was all interwoven. It was only naive innocence that made people believe that criminals were a different breed, that there were 'good people' and 'bad people' and that never the twain would meet.

The question facing Vishnu now was what to do.

He told his sister Menaka to go back home and stay quiet about the matter. It was imperative she not speak of Chandra or his arrest to anyone else aloud. Not even their parents; especially not their parents. For all his intelligence on intellectual matters, their father was not attuned to the more sordid side of the world. He would blunder into the palace guard's headquarters, demanding that Chandra be released at once or questioning why the boy had been arrested. That would be a fatal mistake, for himself and for Vishnu's mother and sisters. To question was to threaten, and to threaten was to commit an unforgivable offence—not only against the law and authority of Pataliputra but against Magadha itself.

Pundit Gupta would end up in the same reeking dungeon where Chandra lay, never to return home. And as a result of his indiscretion, his wife and daughters would be declared fair game for all takers, to do with and dispose of as they desired.

Vishnu Gupta was not his father.

He was still a boy, barely more than a child, and had no real political influence or wealth or any other advantage to fight the corrupt, venal and omnipotent system that had now absorbed Chandra into its belly.

But he possessed something that was almost as powerful.

Knowledge.

And the will and strength to use that knowledge.

19

'Anyaya!'

Heads turned. Frowns appeared. Guards stepped forward.

'Anyaya!' repeated the voice as the speaker approached the court.

Silence began to fall in stages over the gathering of nobles and courtiers. Even the prisoners huddled in their chains in one corner peered in bleak curiosity. The Emperor was speaking to one of his many queens, saying something that had caused her to blush—most certainly something unrelated to actual court proceedings—and as the speaker approached the area before the main imperial dais, he broke off his sweet mutterings and frowned down with his imperious gaze. The last person to pay any notice to the intrusion was the man at the centre of the court, the impressario in charge of this opulent circus, Maha-amatya Rakshasa himself.

He was speaking to a group of his aides, giving them instructions in a combination of coded words and hand gestures that only they could interpret. He finished whatever he was saying and then deigned to turn, slowly and with his perennial dignity, to view the intruder rapidly approaching within speaking distance of the dais.

'Anyaya! Ghor anyaya!' said the speaker.

A host of palace guards advanced upon the speaker, spears pointed, ready to prod, poke, pierce, penetrate, pin, and penalise.

The delegation of visiting foreign dignitaries standing nearby gasped and raised their hands to their mouths, fascinated yet horrified at the sight of more than a dozen armed men preparing to commit violence upon what to them appeared to be only a little child.

Vishnu stood calmly in the midst of the forest of spears, palms joined together in the universal gesture of appeal, his little face and bald pate smooth, innocent and open.

The palace guards converged upon him, lowering their spears to account for the unexpected height difference. They had guarded children before, but never one this young or this small. It was a first in their experience. To all those gathered in the imperial court of Magadha that day, it was a first as well. They had never heard of nor seen a child stride into court with the unshakeable confidence and authority of this little brahmin boy.

Samrat Mahapadma Nanda looked down imperiously from his throne. Even his jaded eyes were fractionally intrigued: this was something new. It was hard these days for the Emperor to view anything genuinely new. He had done it all, seen it all, experienced it all. But not this: never before had he seen a little child storm into his court and shout at the top of his voice.

Anyaya.

Injustice.

Whatever did the little fellow mean?

It was intriguing enough for him to wonder.

The Emperor's curiosity was aroused. This did not happen often.

He glanced once at the Maha-amatya.

Maha-amatya's famously inexpressive face did not react: the legend was that nobody had ever seen him show emotion, any emotion.

Were those who knew him permitted to guess, they might have suggested that at that instant, the Maha-amatya appeared somewhat peeved. Not that his face revealed this reaction. But the irate way he gestured to his aides did suggest peevishness. Then again, he might simply have been curt. The Prime Minister was almost always curt, except when he was vehement.

He gestured peevishly.

The aides passed on the order.

The guards who had converged on the intruder immediately lifted their spears, raising them to point upwards at the elaborately decorated ceiling. They took a step backwards, away from the little brahmin boy, then retreated back still further, to resume their posts. If required again, they were still only a few yards away, while the intruder himself was a good twenty yards from the actual person of the Emperor, and perhaps eighteen yards from the person of the Maha-amatya. And if urgently required, spears could also be flung. But they did not anticipate such actions. It was a mere boy after all; a brahmin child at that. Empty handed and with no place on his flimsy white garments to conceal a weapon, even if he even knew how to use such a weapon. He posed no threat to anyone.

Or so it seemed.

The Maha-amatya made a second gesture to his aides.

One of them turned to Vishnu and rattled off a standard disclaimer about the proper protocol for approaching the court and the Emperor and Maha-amatya, and about the correct manner in which to address them. The aide ended this longish soliloquy with the single word: 'Speak.'

Vishnu bowed his head, his palms still joined. He bowed his head so low that from the perspective of the imperial dais, only his chotti was visible upon his bald head.

The sight evoked some amusement from the queens and princesses seated on the dais. Even the princes, who were rarely amused by anything that transpired in court, looked up to scowl down at the sight. The Empress, in particular, was highly amused by the sight. Delighted might not be the worst way to describe her pleasure. 'How sweet,' she said to the Emperor, who blinked, then cracked his painted lips to smile garishly at her. He was in an amorous mood that afternoon and had been flirting with his first wife, the Empress, for the sheer novelty of the experience. He could not recall the last time he had romanced his Empress. It would be almost like having a new woman. He was pleased by her amusement. He recalled now that amusement always put her in the mood for amorous activity. This was what made him smile back at her. He hardly glanced at the source of her amusement: the little chotti on the little bald head bent low before the imperial dais.

Not unaware of the effect, Vishnu straightened up to his full height of some three feet and said in his clear but slightly lisping tone: 'Maha-amatya, Samrat, this is anyaya. Gross injustice.'

The Empress raised her perfectly shaped brows, amused even more by the lisping tone.

The truth was, Vishnu did not usually lisp. He had been afflicted by the slight softness of pronunciation when he had first learned to speak, at the ripe old age of seventeen months. When he was older—and in Vishnu's case, unlike other people, that meant a period of months not years—he saw that his lisping caused much amusement in his sisters, and even indulgent smiles from his mother, while his father frowned.

These reactions were interpreted by his little developing brain and correctly surmised to be not the correct responses to the actual words he had spoken. He had soon learned to overcome his natural tendency and within days was able to speak without any lisp. His family had attributed the change in his speech to normal development, but in fact, it took special effort on Vishnu's part to pronounce each word without his natural lisping. The cause of the lisp was physical: a slight extension of his palette which resulted in the softening of consonants. He had maintained his lispless speech to this day, but on the occasion of his appearance before the Imperial Court, he allowed his vocal muscles to lapse back into their natural state and allowed the lisp to reveal itself once more. Despite the softening of the consonants, his words were quite clear and comprehensible, but the combination of the lisp with his impressive vocabulary and eloquence, small stature, precious age, and his immaculate appearance resembling a full-grown adult brahmin right down to the wooden cleats on his tiny feet, produced a very unique effect. It was like watching a large doll speaking.

Even the eldest prince, Dhana Nanda, who happened to be present in court that day, was intrigued. Dhana Nanda possessed many dolls, some almost as large as himself, and he was a little larger than Vishnu Gupta. To him, as to the rest of his family and the court, Vishnu Gupta was like a living brahmin doll, a diminutive effigy of a full-grown brahmin pundit, speaking and expressing himself with the impressive vocabulary and style of a learned pundit. It was an extraordinary sight and it amused Dhana Nanda enormously.

He laughed aloud.

His mother, the Empress, frowned at him. For an instant, she feared that he was in one of his moods. Everyone feared Dhana Nanda's moods, including his own mother. But she saw that he was smiling and looking pleased. Dhana Nanda clapped his hands together and said, 'Speak! Speak! Little Pundit!'

The courtiers looked at each other, unsure of how to react.

The Emperor laughed.

The Empress laughed as well.

The Queens and princesses and princes laughed too.

The nobles and courtiers laughed too.

The visiting foreign dignitaries looked around, unable to fully comprehend the reason for the laughter. Their translators shrugged and laughed as well. The dignitaries followed their example and laughed along.

Even the guards frowned and smiled uncertainly.

The prisoners were the only ones who stared coldly around, wondering, not for the first time, if all rich and powerful people were insane. Based on the evidence of their miserable lives and this spectacle, it would appear so. Stark, raving bonkers.

The Maha-amatya stared hawkishly at the cause of this merriment, the little, life-size doll-genius standing before the imperial dais. He did not laugh. Neither did his aides, though some of them may have wanted to laugh; if they did so, they laughed inside, and hid it well. They had learned from a master at concealing emotions, especially the most human emotion of all: joy.

For his part, Vishnu bowed again, showing the imperial dais his chotti and bald head once more.

This provoked further peals of laughter.

Which set the court off again.

Finally, when the amusement had run its course and the court had subsided, he nodded, and resumed his petition.

'I bow to your imperial wisdom and ask you, my Emperor, my Maha-amatya, should adharma and anyaya be permitted to exist within your purview?'

The Emperor frowned, leaning forward. Had the little pundit asked a question? What exactly was the question? Had he missed something.

Maha-amatya gestured.

An aide asked: 'What do you speak of? Come to the point quickly. The court's time is valuable and not to be wasted on frivolity.'

In other words: Which specific case of injustice do you mean? There are so many, we could be here all year, listing them all out.

But of course, not in so many words.

Vishnu bowed just his head this time.

'I speak of the unjustly accused prisoner incarcerated in the Maha-amatya's dungeons.'

At soon as he said these words, a silence fell over the courtroom. Every courtier in the chamber reacted with widened eyes and a sharp intake of breath. Those words sounded very much like a challenge to the Maha-amatya, delivered directly to his face. How could the Minister of Justice be responsible for 'unjustly' arresting and imprisoning anyone? To suggest such a thing was treasonous. And the penalty for treason was immediate execution.

So self-evident was this fact that the aide addressing Vishnu was about to say so aloud. But to his utter astonishment, his own master, the Maha-amatya, spoke instead.

'Young man,' he said. 'You are my pupil and protege. I admire your intelligence and talent. As you know, nyaya, the dispensing of justice, is a complex and difficult subject that takes a lifetime to master. Why do you trouble your little mind with such matters? Leave these troubles to us adults to manage. The Emperor's Court has many demands and matters to hear and the day is wearing on. Go now. Run along and play with your companions. You have been studying very hard of late, and no doubt you are wearied and stressed by your efforts. You are still a child and children need their play.'

All this was said in a kindly patronising tone, just like an uncle might say to a nephew. It was so unlike the Maha-amatya to speak like this that many regular courtiers as well as all the aides stole quick glances to see if it was him speaking. The tone as well as the words befuddled everyone in court, except a few.

It was for the benefit of these few that the Maha-amatya had used this ploy. The Emperor and his family, as well as the visiting royal dignitaries, were all imperials, and as such they expected people in their presence to behave nobly and honourably. Never mind that such displays might be only posturing for effect; one did not expose the ugly, dark truth of imperialism in the presence of imperials.

The lord of the manor wanted the illusion that he was a great and noble lord to be maintained in his presence: even if, the instant his back was turned, the abuse and exploitation continued viciously. The uglier the reality, the more beautiful the pretense. Why do the very rich and powerful crave ostentatious displays of their own wealth and luxury, why do they love pristine white decor? Because they want everyone to remember that they are rich and powerful; and because pristine walls prove that no blood is spilled in their presence. How can anything bad be happening when everything looks so clean and beautiful? How can people who look so noble and richly dressed behave in any way but nobly and immaculately?

Maha-amatya was performing this charade because of the earlier reactions of the Emperor and his family. They had been amused and entertained by Vishnu's looks and manner. To attack this little boy, a brahmacharya doll in appearance, would make him look cruel and tyrannical, and that in turn would reflect on the imperial family as well. His job in such cases was to smile, preen and speak sweetly, but firmly and usher the troublesome pest out of the court, to be dealt with brutally and mercilessly by his men acting on his orders, but in private. This was why dungeons were deep underground, why jails had no windows on public streets, why torture houses were dark houses in remote corners.

Maha-amatya meant to dispel Vishnu the way he might flick an insect off his shoulder. Leaving it to his aides or guards to grab and quash. He did not get his hands dirty, or sully the imperial presence. Not for a mere brahmin child.

Vishnu smiled and addressed Maha-amatya directly. His lisp became a tad more pronounced, his speech and body language even more appealing and amusing. The game was on!

'You are too kind, Maha-amatyaji. But it is from you that I have learned the tiny smattering of knowledge of law during my brief presence in Pataliputra. By your grace, and under your tutelage, I have become aware of this matter of grave injustice being committed without your knowledge. And as such, I felt compelled to bring it to your attention. As you yourself taught us, any injustice committed in this empire, particularly in this, the heart of the empire, is an affront to the Emperor himself. Injustice is treasonous and the penalty for treason is swift execution!'

Prince Dhana Nanda clapped his hands again, laughing. 'Little pundit. Speak more! Speak more! We like him speaking. Say something else to Mamatya!'

The Empress smiled indulgently at her eldest son and heir to the empire. His father, the Emperor, was not as indulgent and wanted to tell the prince to shut up so he could try to make sense of what was going on, but he had learned from experience that Dhana was best left alone. The prince had once punched his own father in the nose, then bit him on the waist, all because his father had told him to be quiet for a while as he was speaking to an important person. Dhana Nanda had been only three years old at that time, and since then, he had found considerably more violent ways to express himself. Mahapadma Nanda knew this well, because almost every few months he had to call on Maha-amatya to clean up the aftermath of those periodic 'expressions' of the prince's inner feelings. He had no desire to provoke such an expression right now in full open court.

He leaned forward, trying to understand what exactly the Maha-amatya and the little pundit were discussing. It appeared to him as if they were engaged in a private debate that had been going on for a while, one he had only just begun listening to. He could make no sense of what they were debating.

'Yes,' he said now, raising his voice before the Maha-amatya could respond to Vishnu Gupta. 'Yes, my son is right. Let us hear more of what the little pundit is saying. Little brahmin, what is this injustice of which you speak and who is this person who is wrongly incarcerated in the dungeons?'

Maha-amatya stiffened at the sound of the Emperor's voice. He would have ignored the young prince's outburst, knowing his impulsiveness and childish behaviour all too well. But he could not ignore the Emperor. However powerful the Prime Minister may be, he could never speak against the Emperor, not even a word. It was this very fact that Vishnu Gupta had been counting on and it was the reason for his dramatic entrance and cryptic words. The moment the Emperor spoke, he knew he had achieved his first goal. He had superseded Maha-amatya without causing any offence or arguing with him personally.

Vishnu replied meekly and with the same pronounced lisp: 'Your Imperial Majesty, I apologise for not being sufficiently clear. Forgive my lapse and forgive me also if I have seemed rude or abrupt in any way. I am only a child and only eager to put to the test the lessons I have learned from Maha-amatya himself.'

'Indeed,' the Emperor replied. 'Your answer and your manner please me greatly. You have not caused any offence with your words or manner. How can a mere child offend the Emperor of Magadha? Please, go on. Explain yourself.'

Vishnu bowed again, prompting another burst of delighted laughter from Prince Dhana Nanda. 'You are too kind, Your Imperial Highness. I speak of a youth named Chandra who is arrested and placed in the Maha-amatya's dungeons.'

The Emperor frowned. 'Why does this youth matter to you?'

Vishnu bowed again. 'He is my brother-in-law.'

A ripple of murmurs passed across the courtroom. This was getting interesting. By the Maha-amatya's own unspoken rules, if one member of a family was found to have given offence to the Empire, all members of the family were considered equally guilty. But never before had a little child presented a case, and never before had such a person been the personal protege of the Maha-amatya himself. Now, everyone was as intrigued as the Emperor and the Imperial Family to see how this turned out. Bets began to be placed discreetly, on the outcome of the case. The odds were entirely in favour of the little pundit losing.

'That is unfortunate,' the Emperor said with a frown. 'Because as you may be aware, treason is a family offence.'

'Indeed, Your Imperial Majesty, I am aware of this fact,' said Vishnu, lisping endearingly. 'I have learned as much from the Maha-amatya. This is why I present myself to the court. As it is my very own brother-in-law who is accused of the crime, I believe that I too, and all my family members are equally guilty in the eyes of the law.'

The quantum of the bets increased, doubled, tripled, quadrupled, as everyone saw that the little pundit had just dug a very deep hole for himself from which nobody could possibly escape. The odds dropped dramatically, since the punters felt that the outcome was a foregone conclusion.

'Do you realise what you are saying, little pundit?' The Emperor was frankly surprised. This was turning out to be quite an invigorating day after all. He had never encountered such a case before. 'Maha-amatya, does your protege realise the consequences of such a statement?'

Maha-amatya was staring dumbly at Vishnu Gupta. For once, he appeared to have nothing to say. At the Emperor's question, he blinked twice, then looked in his liege's direction as protocol demanded. 'He is a child, sire. Surely he is wearied from too much studying. I do not think he knows what he speaks of.'

'I do!' said Vishnu, shouting suddenly, as if he had lost his patience. He stamped his foot hard, producing a ringing echo. 'I demand justice. I know the penalty for treason is swift execution. I wish to be judged for my brother-in-law's crime and receive a verdict immediately.'

All of a sudden, he was behaving like a typical seven-year-old who had lost his temper and was having an outburst.

Even Prince Dhana Nanda rose to his feet and stamped his feet, shouting in agreement, 'Little Pundit wants. Give him his want!'

Many in the court shook their heads, feeling sorry for the little brahmin who had clearly lost his mind.

The Emperor shook his head too. 'Little guru, Maha-amatya is right. You are merely a child. You cannot fully understand what you are saying. If what you say is true, and your brother-in-law is indeed guilty, then you would be guilty too, and you as well as your entire family would be executed under law.'

Vishnu nodded slowly, breathing deeply as if to calm himself. Then said, 'Forgive my behaviour, I apologise again. It is a personal matter and very vital to me. I mis-spoke earlier. I understand the law and the penalty for the crime of treason. But I believe my brother-in-law and my entire family to be innocent. We are loyal citizens of Your Imperial Highness and would never do or say anything treasonous. On the contrary, this is all the work of another person who has falsely accused my brother-in-law and implicated my family as a result. That is why I came here to throw myself on your mercy. It is anyaya. Injustice. And I come to you now seeking justice.'

Maha-amatya shook his long bony finger slowly. 'This is untenable. Young Vishnu Gupta, you are surely unaware of what you are saying. I—'

'One moment, Maha-amatyaji,' the Emperor said gently.

Maha-amatya stopped and looked back. He bowed his head contritely. 'Of course, Your Imperial Highness. It is your court, I am merely your servant.'

He turned to face the court again, looking as he always did. Only his closest aides could see the barely suppressed rage growing within him. He concealed it as artfully as ever.

'Now, young pundit,' the Emperor said, 'From what I understand, you are saying that your brother-in-law is innocent and someone else falsely implicated him. Why would anyone do such a thing?'

'To escape execution, Your Imperial Highness,' Vishnu replied.

'Of course. That is perfectly logical. But who is this person who you claim framed your relative, and who you say is actually guilty of the crime? Do you know this person's identity.'

Vishnu nodded his head vigorously, his chotti bouncing up and down, amusing Dhana Nanda further. 'I do, Your

Imperial Majesty. He is right here in the court at this moment. There he is.'

And Vishnu pointed at one of Maha-amatya's closest aides.

The court was startled into a variety of reactions. The odds changed and so did the bets, but almost all remained against Vishnu. Only a few outliers, for the sake of variety, bet on him, just on the grounds that he had lasted this long, perhaps he could last a little longer.

'That is one my closest aides,' Maha-amatya said stiffly. 'How dare you accuse him!'

The Emperor sat back, intrigued. A sly smile appeared on his face. He had begun to see something he had never seen before: an antagonist who could get under the skin of the Maha-amatya. That itself was very unusual. The fact that it was a seven-year-old boy was remarkable. He was eager to see how this played out now.

'Can you prove your allegation?' the Emperor asked.

Vishnu Gupta nodded again. 'I can. My own sister heard that brahmin say treasonous words against your Imperial Highness.' He turned to look directly at the Maha-amatya. 'As well as against the Maha-amatya himself.'

'And what was the nature of this treasonous statement?' the Emperor asked. He raised his hand quickly. 'You need not repeat the actual words. Merely give the court some idea of the nature of their content.'

Vishnu paused as if thinking hard. He scratched his bald head, and finally said, 'I will not repeat the exact words for they would cause offence. But he said very bad things about Prince Dhana Nanda.'

'About...,' The Emperor started from his throne, then looked at his son and heir.

Dhana Nanda grinned and pointed at Vishnu. 'My name.

He said my name.' He clapped his hands again. 'I like little pundit. He will be my friend.'

A tiny hint of a frown appeared on Maha-amatya's face. His eyes cut sideways to glance at the aide in question. A train of thought began to pass through his mind, going back to the day when he had discovered that particular bad mess in the Prince's chambers and had asked the servants and maids to clean it up and find the Prince a new kitten. The Prince had long since killed that second kitten too, finally tiring of its companionship and eliminating the need to replace it. The aide who had been present with the Maha-amatya that day had in fact been this very aide, which meant that he had some knowledge of what had transpired in the Prince's chambers. There was a connection, and such a connection could not be coincidental. He looked at Vishnu with fresh eyes, wondering for the first time if there was some truth to what the little pundit was saying.

The aide saw the change in the Maha-amatya's face and panicked. 'My Lord! This boy is lying. The thief Chandra was not even arrested for treasonous comments. He was arrested because we learned that he was behind the murders of two of our men in the Gate Sector.'

'Silence!' Maha-amatya thundered. 'You will speak only when spoken to!'

Vishnu bowed again, addressing the Maha-amatya. 'Maha-amatyaji, my sister also heard him say that he was the one who had those two men killed. He was boasting about it to Chandra and telling him how he knew all about...,' Vishnu paused, 'about certain things to do with Prince Dhana Nanda that I will not mention here, and because of his knowledge he could influence the Maha-amatya if he wished. He was boasting; Chandra grew angry and slapped him and told him he was a traitor to the Emperor and to Maha-amatya and should be dragged up before the court for punishment. But the aide had Chandra arrested instead and then told you, Maha-amatya, that it was Chandra who had killed the two men. He did not mention anything about the Prince because then you would know that it was he who had spoken about it.'

The Emperor spoke into the sudden silence that followed these words. 'How can we know that you are telling the truth? Or that your sister was telling the truth? Or that Chandra is telling the truth?'

Vishnu nodded again and said, 'How else would I, my sister, or my brother-in-law have learned about the matter pertaining to Prince Dhana Nanda except through Maha-amatya's aide?'

An even longer silence followed this.

Finally, it was Maha-amatya Rakshasa who spoke.

'The young pundit has spoken the truth. Based on what he has said just now, I am satisfied that it was in fact my own aide, this traitor, who said treasonous things about our noble prince and heir.'

'I spoke when I was drunk, Master! Please forgive me!' the aide cried out, further sealing his fate.

Maha-amatya gestured and the same guards who had converged on Vishnu Gupta earlier, now rushed to encircle the aide. They immediately escorted him off the imperial dais and to a safe distance.

'Then this would mean that the young pundit's brother-in-law is innocent of treason,' the Emperor said thoughtfully.

The Maha-amatya took a moment to reply, his long avian jaw working tightly. 'It would seem so, yes.'

'Your Imperial Highness,' Vishnu said. 'I ask that my brother-in-law be freed at once and exonerated of all charges.'

The Emperor nodded and said quietly to the Maha-amatya. 'See that it is done.'

Maha-amatya gestured and another of his aides rushed to carry out his orders.

The Emperor rose to his feet. 'We shall now retire for a brief respite,' he said.

The rest of the Imperial family rose with him. Only Prince Dhana Nanda remained seated.

'Dhana?' said his mother, smiling at him hopefully.

Prince Dhana Nanda pointed at Vishnu Gupta. 'I want him to be my friend. Little Pundit.'

Maha-amatya had been standing brooding silently. Now he turned to Prince Dhana Nanda and smiled. 'Yes, of course. As you wish, young Master.'

Maha-amatya walked down from the dais to where Vishnu Gupta stood. He towered above the little brahmin by several feet. He had to lean downwards to place his long bony fingers on Vishnu's slender shoulder.

'It seems you have won your first case and also made a new friend. Go now, accompany the Crown Prince. You are both the same age. I am sure you will find many things in common. He loves to play games and so do you. You will have much joy together. Go play with him. Play a good game.'

He smiled, revealing his long yellow teeth to Vishnu. 'But remember, when playing with emperors and princes, you must play by their rules, not your own.'

Then he laughed aloud, as if he had said something very amusing, and turned away.

His laughter echoed in Vishnu Gupta's ears.

Acknowledgements

Gautam Padmanabhan, for his unwavering support and championing of my work over the years. While to so many working at multi-national publishing houses in India, their job is just that, for Gautam Padmanabhan, the business of books is far more than a business. And it shows. In Westland's continued success and the success of his authors. He is truly The Prince of Indian Publishing. Gautam, you deserve every success and I wish you many more to come.

Sanghamitra Biswas, yet again, does a fine job of editing the book and overseeing it through the publication pipeline. She is a dream editor to work with and I would wish any author an editor of her high calibre.

The entire team at Westland, for all their yeoman service. You rock!

Thank you also to my amazing readers—this means you!—who have supported and encouraged me through the many long years and difficulties involved with any writing career. Especially those who subscribed to my ebooks website www.akbebooks.com and enabled me to continue writing these books. They are the real heroes of this and every epic I write: thank you!

If you like this book or any other book by me, then please show your love:

Write positive comments on social media.

Leave good reviews and ratings on Goodreads, Amazon, and anywhere else you wish.

Spread the word by telling other readers about my books.

Without your support, none of this would be possible! Thank you and Happy Reading!

THE CHANAKYA TRILOGY

By Ashok K. Banker

BOOK 2

COMING SOON

ONLY FROM

Westland Books